LIVING SPRINGS PUBLISHERS PRESENTS:

STORIES THROUGH THE AGES
BABY BOOMERS PLUS
2023

Compiled and edited by:
Henry E. Peavler, Dan Peavler, and
Jacqueline Veryle Peavler

Introduction by: Henry Peavler and Dan Peavler

Short Stories by:
J.R. Reynolds, Robert Robeson, Bill Weatherford,
Brad Bennett, Jeannette M. Bond, Raymond Brunt,
Patti Ann Pecina, JD Clapp, Sarah Elizabeth Das Gupta,
Edward E. Douglas, Ellen Herbert, George Koyl,
Michail Mulvey, Bill Smoot, Susan M Pomerantz,
Thom Schilling, Elizabeth Taylor-Mead, Cheryl Velasquez

Paperback ISBN: **978-1-953686-31-2**
Paperback ISSN: 2770-0178
eBook ISBN: 978-1-953686-32-9
eBook ISSN: 2770-0194

www.LivingSpringsPublishers.com

Cover design by Jacqueline Peavler
Cover photo taken by Tina Sutton in Byers, Colorado.
All rights reserved.

Dedicated to the past that shaped our present.

Contents

Autumn Leaves Falling 1

    J.R. Reynolds 9

Heading Home—A Prisoner of War at Christmas.....10

    Robert Robeson 26

Drawknife 27

    Bill Weatherford..44

The Faller...45

    Brad Bennett 68

The Good Things Consignment Shop 69

    Jeannette M. Bond..92

The Reunion..93

    Raymond Brunt 107

Beholden to the Sea...108

    JD Clapp...122

Drums of War and of Memory Eighty years on from World War 11 123

    Sarah Elizabeth Das Gupta...................................134

The Password 135

    Edward E. Douglas..150

The Men in the Dunes 151

    Ellen Herbert 165

Blank Page..166

    George Koyl..182

Lunch at the Sad Cafeteria 183

    Michail Mulvey...201

Hamburger Girl 202

    Patti Ann Pecina 217

Dirge... 218

    Susan M. Pomerantz 227

Killer at Kozy Kove Kampground 228

    Thom Schilling...244

The Way It Had to Be... 245

    Bill Smoot 264

Grace... 265

    Elizabeth Taylor-Mead 277

The Last Word... 278

    Cheryl Velasquez 288

Living Springs Publishers 289

Synopses

Autumn Leaves Falling: First place in this year's Baby Boomers Plus goes to J. R. Reynolds. His poignant story of two brothers with a very special bond will melt the coldest of hearts. "Pete was special; he didn't have to grow up." This beautiful thought sets the stage for what follows. Pete and Jerry experience life to the fullest and make many wonderful friends along the way. This story will make your day.

Heading Home—A Prisoner of War at Christmas: This story won second place in this year's contest. A well-written account of a Vietnam veteran returning from that unpopular war to find protesters in the airport on his arrival. Again, a story that needs to be told for those who don't know. The ending is a touching surprise that ties the whole narrative together. Don't miss this one written by Robert Robeson.

Drawknife: The third-place winner in this year's contest is a beautifully written story about a boy's relationship with his grandfather. Oh, how wonderful it would be if we all could have an adult in our life like, Fredrick Haarm Telkamp. This is a fast paced, well-crafted story that keeps our attention throughout. A must read from Bill Weatherford.

The Faller by Brad Bennett: A horrible event in World War II has unforeseen repercussions for many people through the years, long after the war itself. Our narrator, Brad, nicknamed Sonny, leads a difficult life moving from one place to the next and not realizing until he is well into adulthood the reasons for the hardships. An excellent story of human frailty and strength.

The Good Things Consignment Shop: Lynn and Joe Miller own a consignment shop in a small town. Jeannette M. Bond has written a wonderfully entertaining tale about old and new clients who often get a lot more than they bargained for as Lynn looks for opportunities to ply her matchmaking skills. A fun and charming story, well worth your time to read.

The Reunion: A short story written in second person narration about a man who has avoided going to a high school reunion for decades. He chooses this particular reunion to attend and discovers what he has missed, both good and bad. But it's really a story about grief, and existential angst, and how people deal with each of these emotions differently. Raymond Brunt, has crafted a unique and witty story about a subject we face at one time or another...growing old.

Beholden to the Sea: Two men are winding down a fishing trip in the open waters of the Pacific, 22 miles from shore. Suddenly the boat is destroyed as it crashes into an unseen obstacle. Only one man survives. His extraordinary story of perseverance and luck is described with spine-tingling accuracy by author, JD Clapp. This is a must read.

Drums of War and of Memory Eighty years on from World War 11: Sarah Elizabeth Das Gupta gives us a personal memoir of a childhood in the Surrey countryside in the immediate aftermath of World War 2. Ironically a war-scarred landscape becomes the playground of the local gang of 'war-babies'. They roam the woods armed with gas masks and bottles of Tizer, meet in underground war shelters and interpret secret codes in the whispering pine woods. This is a story waiting eighty years to be told which endorses the spirit of survival.

The Password: The setting is World War II...Germany. Our heroes, a young boy, and his grandfather, are part of the underground, the resistance. The risks they take and the things they do are justified because the information they possess is of vital importance to the Allied cause. This is an exciting story full of suspense and intrigue by Edward E. Douglas. Don't miss it.

The Men in the Dunes by Ellen Herbert: It's 1967 and our heroine, Ellen, has received reluctant permission from her father to join a military family on a beach excursion near Camp LeJeune, Jacksonville, North Carolina. The Vietnam War is raging but the Sergeant, his family and Ellen are staying in a cottage on the beach. Just one problem -don't leave the cottage after dark. Read the story to find out why.

Blank Page: Bill Morris receives a letter that contains a blank sheet of paper. A mystery that only one person can unravel. The journey to the surprise ending is full of suspense and anticipation. Author, George Koyl, does a wonderful job of maintaining the pace and keeping our interest until the very end. Is it a happy ending? You have to judge for yourself.

Lunch at the Sad Cafeteria: The setting for this story is a second-grade classroom three days before Christmas vacation, 1955. Michael, the narrator, is battling his arch-enemy, a fellow classmate named Margaret. Despite their hatred for each other, the two share a common hatred for their teacher, Miss Cronin. They also share a hunger for love and simple sustenance. The two are forced to band together against their classmates who seek revenge for the culinary assault on their lunches that takes place in the cloakroom. You need to read this entertaining tale by Michail Mulvey.

Hamburger Girl: Author Patti Ann Pecina has crafted a heart-warming story about an episode revolving around drive-in movie night. It is 1967, and despite the title the story really hinges on a fish sandwich gone horribly wrong. This story will make you laugh, but at the same time, the ending is a wonderful example of a family coming together in crisis.

Dirge: Author, Susan M. Pomerantz has crafted a marvelous story of a tragedy seen through the eyes of a 14-year-old girl. Our heroine, Kendra, is both a realist and a romantic who reads more than her mother thinks proper. She is forced to help her father with the other children as her mother's health deteriorates. The ending is heart wrenching yet full of promise. This is a beautifully written, touching story. Don't miss it.

Killer at Kozy Kove Kampground: A mystery unfolds as the family leaves for a vacation across the southeastern United States. Thom Schilling has written a wonderful story of intrigue and misadventure that leaves you laughing and shaking your head at the same time. Who is the shadowy stranger in the foreboding campground far from the beaten path? Find out for yourself.

The Way it Had to Be: It is 1962. Danny is a new reporter at his hometown newspaper when a black man is shot by a policeman one night in the town stockyards. The policeman's story is thin, and Danny tries to rally the paper with the few who are seeking justice. The prevailing winds are blowing in a different direction. Bill Smoot has given us a timely and well-written account of dealing with an issue charged with emotions of all kinds. Read it!

Grace: This is a wonderful story about a strong-willed woman narrated through the eyes of her granddaughter. "Grace Adams Macaluso was a wildcat..." we learn early in the tale. Living poor but happy in "one of the more respectable parts of Brooklyn, New York." The author, Elizabeth Taylor-Mead, keeps us interested throughout the story. An uplifting story that you don't want to miss.

The Last Word: The siblings gather as the last few hours of their father's life unfolds. Many stories are shared...some funny, some poignant and some surprising. Author, Cheryl Velasquez, has written a beautifully crafted ode to the emotions we, as humans, feel upon the changes in our lives and how it's not always important to have the last word.

Introduction

Living Springs Publishers is happy to announce the winners of the **Stories Through the Ages Baby Boomers Plus 2023** short story contest. This is our seventh annual contest for authors born in 1966 or before. French novelist and essayist Marcel Proust wrote, "We don't receive wisdom; we must discover it for ourselves after a journey that no one can take for us or spare us." The knowledge, experience and insight this seasoned group of authors share to the world in this year's book, by way of imaginative and creative stories, makes the 2023 edition a must read for those who enjoy short stories.

As our contest grows in popularity globally, we find that people, no matter where they come from, experience the same sorrows and joys. Humankind has many more similarities than we have differences. The authors in the book give us a glimpse into moments in life where people laughed and cried, endured and succeeded, hated and loved. No matter where we come from or who we are, we can all learn lessons from life and humanities best and worst moments.

We at Living Springs Publishers believe that the happiest people in the world are those with the ability to imagine. Many great ideas began with a dream. Albert Einstein stated, "imagination will take you everywhere." We thank the numerous authors who took the time to write their stories and send them to our contest. As in the previous books we gave the authors the flexibility to stretch their ideas and visions by writing about any subject they wanted too. We hope that those who submitted their creative works enjoyed writing the stories as much as we enjoyed reading them.

Autumn Leaves Falling
By J.R. Reynolds

The doctors tell me I've reached the autumn of my years and it's time to slow down and appreciate the good things in life. As I watch the autumn leaves fall to the ground, I think back to the day I was born. My brother Pete was six years old.

Pete was special; he didn't have to grow up. He lived in the world of an eight-year-old. Some called him retarded, but that was because they never got to know him. He was my hero and my best friend. He woke up happy every day and made everyone who met him happier too. We were inseparable. Wherever I went Pete was right there.

The day I started school was a hard day for Pete. He didn't understand why he couldn't go. No amount of explaining by Mom could make him understand. He sat on the front steps of our house until he saw the school bus coming down the road in the afternoon and ran out to stop it for fear they wouldn't know I was supposed to get off at our house.

Mom promised the bus driver Pete wouldn't run out in front of the bus again. After the first day he never did. But he still sat on the front porch waiting for me until I graduated from high school. While he waited, he would wave and smile at every car traveling past our house.

Over the years people got use to Pete sitting on the porch waving at them. They would honk and wave. If he wasn't on the porch our mom would get phone calls from the neighbors checking to see if Pete was ok.

In the summer Pete and I would lie in the grass and watch the clouds and talk about things kids talk about. Sometimes he would say things that didn't make any sense to me until I got older. Once he said life was like the seasons of the year. Spring is a time of rebirth for the world with its warm spring rains, new plant life and baby animals. The summer is time for growing and spreading our wings to improve the world, making it better for all of those around us. The fall of the year or autumn is harvesting time to gather round us the fruits of our labors and shed our troubles and worries to prepare for winter. Winter is time to curl up and go to sleep letting the earth rejuvenate itself and rest. Winter is the most important time of the year; without winter we couldn't have spring.

He told me friends are like leaves on a tree. The more leaves on a tree the healthier the tree is and the more friends we have the better our lives are. With his willingness to help people and his happy smile Pete collected friends like some people collect stray dogs.

When I turned eight, Pete and I started mowing our parent's yard and taking care of the flowerbeds. Pete was afraid of the power mower because loud noises frightened him, so Dad got him a push mower. I would mow the perimeter of the lawn with the power mower and trim the sidewalks with the edger while Pete would mow the center area. I would show him which plants stayed in the flower beds and which to pull out and his favorite job was to rake up the cut grass and bag it for the garbage man.

On garbage day Pete would take his bags out to the curb and wait for the truck to come. When they stopped, he would smile and wave to the guys and yell, "Thank You" as they pulled away. They looked forward to seeing Pete each week. One day they came up and told him, "Thank you for making our day better," and gave him a candy bar. They continued to bring him a candy bar every week until he stopped waiting for them.

Pete's favorite time of the year was in the fall. He loved to rake up the leaves into big piles and then he and I would run and dive into the middle of the pile scattering leaves all over the yard. He would rake big piles of leaves and hide in the pile and when I'd come looking for him, he would jump out and scare me yelling, "Leaf Attack!"

In the winter we'd shovel the snow off the sidewalk and the driveway, but we would end up with Dad, Mom, Pete and I in a snowball fight. When it was over Pete and I would have to clean it up again.

The next year when I was nine and Pete was 15 our aunt, who lived on the same street as us, asked if Pete and I would take care of her lawn. It wasn't long until we were taking care of nine houses on our street.

Pete and I made a wagon that I could pull behind my bike to haul the equipment in. We made signs for each side of the wagon that said, "Pete and Jerry's Lawn Service." Every time we'd stop at a house to mow the yard Pete would knock on the door and let them know we were there, and he would bring them out and show them our wagon and proudly point to his name and tell them, "That's me!"

That was the summer Pete discovered baseball. Our town had a minor league team called The Middleton Stampede. One afternoon Dad got us tickets to watch them play and Pete found his game. Pete and I were able to buy season tickets with the money we made mowing lawns. In no time he knew each player and what position they played. Our summers were planned around all the home games.

We would start mowing at nine each morning and try to have the first lawn finished in time to make the afternoon game. If it was an evening game, then we would get two lawns done before game time.

On Sundays we didn't mow lawns. That was time for church and singing songs. Pete loved to sing even if he didn't know the words. He would sort of hum with his mouth open. Everyone around us would look over and smile at Pete as he sang with us. After church while Mom was fixing dinner Pete and I would set out on the front porch, and I would read the funny papers and the sports section to him. He wanted to know what the other teams were doing in comparison to the Stampede. On Sunday afternoons Pete and I would go to the park and fish for crappies in the lake. We didn't care if we caught anything or not, it was spending time with each other that was important.

Pete was funny in that he didn't care to watch baseball on TV, and he didn't care what the major leagues were doing. All he was interested in was our team. the Stampede. He knew the batting stats on each player and their histories. For a person who couldn't read he was well educated when it came to the Stampede.

By the end of the season the players were coming over to talk to Pete and me before and after each home game. Pete would be sure to tell them what they did wrong during the game, and he was just as generous with praise for the things they did right as well.

On Pete's eighteenth birthday the Ball Park had a Pete Stover Day and Pete was made an honorary member of the team. They presented him with his own uniform, and we got to sit in the dugout for the entire game. From that day on Pete was the team mascot. Each team member would come and shake

Pete's hand before each game for good luck. The coach told me the players worked harder when they played at home because they knew Pete was up in the stands watching and they didn't want to disappoint him.

One year when they were in the playoffs the coach decided with our parents for us to travel with the team and be at every game to bring them luck. It worked because they won the playoffs and at the end of the last game, they put Pete on their shoulders and carried him out onto the field and crowded around him yelling and cheering.

After I graduated from High School Pete and I rented an apartment two blocks from our parent's house. We continued to do lawn care and had expanded to 22 houses in the area. We had another neighborhood boy named Jeff helping us and we made a good team. I began to notice that Pete wasn't moving as fast as he used to. He was still happy and cheerful and still yelled his head off at the ballgames, but he was slowing down. Sometimes on Sundays instead of going fishing or going for a ride in my car he wanted to stay home and rest.

Three days after Pete's 26th birthday we were raking the leaves at our parents' house. I finished with my area and went looking for Pete to see if he was done. I looked in the front yard but no Pete, so I went around to the back yard, and he wasn't there either. I went into the house and asked my parents if they had seen him, and they said they hadn't. I went out to the front of the house where he had been working and I noticed a large pile of leaves next to the big tree in the front yard. I grinned because I knew what was coming. It was going to be a leaf attack. I started calling for Pete and wandered around the yard looking under bushes and behind trees until I got to the pile of leaves where I snuck up and jumped into the pile yelling Leaf Attack!

Pete was lying in the bed of leaves, and he looked up at me and said, "Good one Jerry, you got me." Then I saw a look come across his face that I'd never seen before. It was of sadness. "Jerry, do you remember when I told you how we are like the trees and change with the seasons. I think it's the winter of my life because I feel like a leaf that's fallen and can't get up."

The ambulance came and took him to the hospital while I drove Mom and Dad. When the doctor came to talk to us, he said there wasn't anything they could do for Pete. He'd lived 15 years longer than anyone expected, now his body was shutting down. I asked if I could see him and the Doctor said, "He's been asking for you."

When I walked into the room he said, "Little Brother, don't look so sad. You know I'm the leader and I always go first to fix a place for you. Wasn't I the first one to get here and I waited for you to be born? You are the one who made my life worth living. We had good times and when the leaves fall from the trees think of me. Remember this is your summer of life. It's time for you to go out and make it as remarkable as you made mine!"

"Tell the team to win a game or two for me, and tell the guys on the garbage truck I said thank you for being my friends."

My Mom and Dad were there when he told us that he was tired and was going to go to sleep. He looked at me and said, "I'll see you in the spring brother." He closed his eyes and never woke up.

J.R. Reynolds

JR lives in Texas with his wife of 51 years. They live on a small farm where he writes every day. He has several short stories in various stages of completion along with two novella's and one novel that is going through the edit process. He meets with people in the surrounding communities encouraging them to write their stories several times a month. He is also a carver, an artist working in oils and acrylics and a potter.

Heading Home—A Prisoner of War at Christmas
By Robert Robeson

"There's no place like home."--Dorothy in The Wizard of Oz.

1430 hours, 24 Dec 70.

My contracted "Freedom Bird" aircraft arrived at the San Francisco, California International Airport in early afternoon. I wanted to change into civilian clothes from my khaki uniform, with my Combat Infantry Badge in place in addition to my Silver Star and Purple Heart service ribbons, before my final flight leg to Denver, Colorado.

When we landed, I had a momentary feeling that I was playing hooky from the graveyards of South Vietnam. I'd been introduced to death and dying for a year. So many of those I'd known and served with would never feel the warmth and love of a mother, father, wife or girlfriend's hug again. I felt blessed to be coming home at Christmas to surprise my parents even though I'd seen and experienced things in that war zone that had the potential to haunt me for a long time.

Before changing my clothes, I first had to retrieve my duffel bag and enemy SKS war trophy rifle from the baggage carrousel. I had to check them again before my final flight to Denver, anyway. As I trudged past shops and bars toward an escalator, a trio of sloppily dressed, undernourished, hippie-types, with long greasy hair, near my own age, fell into step behind me.

"Hey, hey, lookie, lookie," one opined loudly. He was about six inches shorter than me and the apparent spokesman for the group. "Looks like we got us one of them 'baby killing maggots' out of V-I-E-T...Nam. How many innocent women and children are you credited with butchering, general?" He was wearing a sweatshirt that said, "Welcome Home War Criminals."

I glanced over my shoulder, didn't reply and kept walking.

"You should have died in 'Nam, you fascist!" Another one shouted.

"Ho, Ho, Ho Chi Minh, the National Liberation Front

is gonna win," the original troublemaker began to chant. The others picked up this sing-song phrase and began repeating it louder and louder as they closed the distance behind me.

I felt my adrenaline level begin to surge like it had in close combat situations so many times before.

I've always believed that there are lessons to be learned from some of life and humanity's worst moments. War heads my own personal list. Armed conflict causes its participants to reflect on the jagged landscape of the human heart where trouble, fear, pain, bloodshed and death are dominate parts of an infantry soldier's daily existence. It's a world of creative cruelty. Sometimes merely surviving such an environment, and then returning to the supposed safety of one's homeland, can be as easy as attempting to perform a disappearing magic trick in front of a firing squad.

"Grunt" was a label most troops used in referring to those of us who spent long days and nights maneuvering in the jungle, rice paddies and mountains of Southeast Asia during the Vietnam War. We constantly tight-roped the brink between life and death. It was like living in a nightmare that wouldn't allow a person to wake up. These extreme experiences tend to remain forever within the scar tissue of a ground-pounder's mind. The ghosts and memories from that conflict, and what happened afterward, continue to rattle their chains in my psyche over 53 years later.

***

My transition from civilian life to soldier occurred after I graduated from the University of Colorado Denver in Denver, Colorado in 1968. A friend informed me that my draft board number was about to be called since he knew someone who knew someone else on the board. I was single, 22 years old and in great physical shape from being a baseball player there and a brown belt in karate, so I decided to enlist before my number was called in an attempt to stay out of the infantry.

I asked my Army recruiter to sign me up as a helicopter door gunner. The potential extra flight pay was important to me and my reluctance to trudge through jungle, swamps, rice paddies and mountains teeming with a large variety of poisonous snakes, leeches, tigers and tropical diseases that were as deadly as the enemy.

Another important fact was that I wouldn't have to function like a pack mule for an entire year's tour, even though I was 6-1 and 205 pounds. Toting a 70–80-pound ammunition and equipment load up and down remote mountains in scorching 100-degree heat and monsoon rains, like a domestic animal, wasn't on my "dream sheet." I'd heard that most flight crews didn't sleep in the field like "hippies" or the homeless but were clustered around airfields where there were bunks and a roof over their heads. They also had ready access to a mess hall and PX, or post exchange, where goodies could be purchased at will to counteract the necessity of living on C-rations like the grunts had to do.

The Army had its own unique and enlightened thoughts about where someone with my educational background needed to be at that time. Most veteran Army personnel were aware that the military had often been administratively proficient at attempting to cram square pegs into round holes through the ages. So, after six months of basic and advanced infantry training at Ft. Benning, Georgia, it cut MOS (military occupational specialty) orders for me as an 11B infantry grunt with a direct line to combat duty in Vietnam. This was a country I couldn't have pointed out on a map in the beginning. That was my initial introduction to the real world of military logic. Or illogic!

I arrived at the Americal Division headquarters in South Vietnam's I Corp operational area on December 24, 1968, and was welcomed in a heartbeat with open arms and an M-16 rifle, since their battalions had recently lost a host of personnel in hit and run battles. Bodies needed to be replaced in a hurry to maintain unit strength and integrity. In my assigned company, a few weeks later, our Viet Cong (VC) and North Vietnamese Army (NVA) adversaries were not as encouraging. Each day and night, we were provided an opportunity to make a name for ourselves...posthumously. For months, many of my infantry comrades had been collecting Purple Hearts in the Hiep Duc area, approximately 35 miles southwest of Da Nang. I learned from these veterans that this was a dangerous and painful hobby at best. In time, all of us "newbees" would discover that instincts for survival are very powerful.

I sent my parents a photo of myself reclining on a

wicker lounge on China Beach in Da Nang, with my left thigh wrapped in bandages, during a three-day, in-country R&R in March of 1969. My unit commander granted this brief respite from combat duty after a short stint at the U.S. Army 95th Evacuation Hospital for a bayonet wound in my thigh. The 95th was also located on China Beach. This came after a scary and bloody battle with the 1st VC Regiment that attempted to overrun our company's position when we set up camp for the night in the Que Son Valley east of Hiep Duc. The VC had fixed bayonets and were coming up the hill en masse nose-to-nose. It ended in hand-to-hand combat for some of us, myself included. Though I was stabbed from the side, my attacker quickly discovered he shouldn't have gotten into a bayonet fight with someone carrying an automatic rifle.

I received a Purple Heart, presented by the hospital commander, lying on actual clean sheets in a bed, recovering from this painful wound. A buddy from my squad, who'd been fighting next to me, came by the second day to inform me I'd also been put in for a Silver Star for my actions during that skirmish. I didn't care about any hero medal. I just wanted to get healed up and back out there with my comrades. He brought along the Russian SKS rifle, with its retractable bayonet, that the VC had attempted to kill me with. He'd picked it up when the firefight was over. He said I needed to register it as a war trophy to take home once I got back to our unit.

Later, on China Beach, I wore my faded jungle fatigue pants, with one leg missing, and an olive drab T-shirt with the words "It Don't Mean Nothin'!" printed in black letters on the front over a red map outline of Vietnam. I figured this photo would prove to my parents that I was still alive.

The one piece of knowledge upon which my fellow soldiers and I could anchor our hopes, and gauge our progress through our one-year tour, was the date each man became eligible to return home. Every Army soldier was assigned a personal DEROS date (date of expected return home from overseas), with the understanding that once you had fulfilled this obligatory 365 days, you'd be returned to the States.

Although the tantalizing promise of home evoked an intense desire to survive--"to make it"--at the same time it fueled a long-suppressed fear that I might not. This sense of vulnerability awakened a paranoia that, in the latter days of my tour, something might come between me and my long-awaited flight home on a silvery "Freedom Bird." We lived in an uncertain environment where we were all potential "bullet and shrapnel stoppers." The most enduring tests faced by each of us was seeing friends killed, wounded and constantly dealing with the unknown. It was something we were forced to accept and make the best of.

Throughout the long middle of my tour, home was a distant dream until I arrived at being a "double-digit midget" (less than 100 days to go). Those of us who spent most of our tours in rice paddies, swamps and jungle were always tired in body and spirit. Many of us were in ill health, having been weakened by wounds, malaria, hepatitis, dysentery or other tropical diseases. This worked in concert with a poor diet, constant sleep deprivation, continuously packing heavy loads in Asian heat and monsoon rain seeking the enemy. We became physically drained. Merely the idea of living long enough to go home served to keep me motivated to hang on until that magic day arrived.

With only a few months to go, I became preoccupied with it. I attempted to believe that I'd probably make it home if nothing untoward happened. This fear that was always there began to slowly overwhelm me. I found myself fighting off thoughts of home which became more prevalent as I got closer. It seemed unreal that I could actually be headed that way after being wounded and surviving the number of ambushes and firefights our unit had encountered. The more similar confrontations occurred, the more I feared something would happen to keep me from seeing those I loved again. I wanted to return home standing up instead of being prostrate in an aluminum casket from the effects of a booby trap, mine, grenade, sniper or satchel charge.

As the days dwindled down to a precious few, every two or three weeks we came in from the field to our base camp to rest and unwind for a few days. That's when transistor radios emerged, and our tents and enlisted club would resound with Armed Forces Radio Network popular music. "Okie from Muskogee," by Merle Haggard in 1969, was one of our favorites. Everyone knew the words and would sing along as we sat around loading up on cold beer or soft drinks, after an eternity of having to drink hot canteen water from often polluted rivers, streams and bomb craters. Halazone tablets had to be added to disinfect this liquid concoction. If not, a grunt paid a heavy price with dysentery and other intestinal maladies. The most popular song of all was "We Gotta Get Outta This Place," by The Animals in 1965. This song was not explicitly written about Vietnam, but the theme became the most popular anthem of the troops I was around.

In my last few months, the military newspaper "Stars and Stripes" began telling about the anti-war marches and demonstrations back in "the World." Most of us could hardly believe some of the stories about how American veterans were being mistreated as they made their way home. Some told how uniformed troops straight off a plane, less than 24-hours out of combat, were being intimidated and harassed at airports and on city streets. Many were spit on, had food thrown at them and were even physically attacked by anti-war college-age malcontents. Others were publicly vilified as "pigs" and "war mongers" during these acts of hatred toward those of us who were ordered to war by our country.

We talked about how ridiculous it seemed and what we'd do if we encountered similar behavior on our way home. We were representing America, following orders from our civilian leaders. The very leaders these protestors had voted into office. We were risking our lives in foreign countries for their government's interests a half-world away. How ungrateful and ignorant could these fellow citizens be?

My DEROS date finally arrived and I said fond farewells to those I'd fought beside for so many months. I gathered my limited possessions in a duffle bag, grabbed my SKS war trophy encased in a fabric gun cover, and caught a helicopter ride to Da Nang for out-processing. A day later, our commercial jet left this war zone behind. My long-awaited "Freedom Bird" had arrived. I was finally heading home, just in time for Christmas.

***

1500 hours, 24 Dec 70.

I stopped as other travelers quickly walked around our group. They pretended not to notice what was going on or what was being said.

"What do you phony 4-F deadbeats know about the National Liberation Front? And you gotta be too poor to afford a haircut. Mommy forget to give you your allowance this week?"

The ringleader had been carrying a chocolate milkshake in one hand and my aggressive comments caused his facial features to redden. I'd purposely targeted this lowlife filled with beatnik bravado in front of his clan of self-righteous clowns.

"Seems Johnny Wayne or Audie Murphy, here, is begging for a thrashing. Right, guys?" He turned toward the others for moral support. Then he suddenly tossed his milkshake at me, drenching my uniform and ribbons.

This smaller antagonist inched even closer and shoved me in the chest.

"Tough guy, huh, paid killer. You ain't brave enough to hurt one of those patriotic North Vietnamese Army heroes!"

Before he had time to react I'd dropped my duffel bag and, with both hands on my covered SKS rifle, butt-stroked him as hard as I could in his solar plexus. He dropped like a mortar round, groaning, gasping for air and ending in a fetal position on the tile floor.

"You pitiful weasels!" I yelled at the other two bedazzled losers as they fled back down the concourse.

Then I headed for the closest restroom to change. *Merry Christmas to me*, I thought later, while sitting alone in the waiting area an hour before my final flight was to leave. Home still seemed far away.

A few minutes later, a middle-aged man and his small son walked up. "Sergeant Peterson, what time is your flight leaving?"

Suspicious about whether they'd witnessed the recent chaos in the terminal concourse, I inquired why he was asking.

"I noticed your duffel bag with your name and rank stenciled on it. We'd like you to stay with us overnight for Christmas dinner tomorrow, if you can't be at your home."

I thanked him but declined the invitation because I didn't want to miss my flight. He said he understood and wished me a "Merry Christmas" before turning to leave with his son.

After they'd taken a few steps, I called out to him and quietly inquired why he asked a perfect stranger to stay at their house for Christmas dinner.

"We lost our oldest son in Vietnam seven months ago and wanted another soldier at our table to celebrate Christmas in his place." For the first time in a very long while, moisture began filling my eyes. Silence fell between us for a few moments.

"Sir, I've changed my mind. I'd love to spend Christmas with your family. I'd have wanted your son to do the same thing for my parents if our positions were reversed. It's the least I can do for a fellow comrade-in-arms. It will be an honor to join you."

The real issue for me had never been whether or not I received a ticker tape parade down main street. Personally, my family and friends telling me it was good to have me home again would be all the welcome I would ever want. But this military family needed to have another soldier fill in for a lost hero son who'd never be able to share this special holiday season with them again.

I remembered the words from an article I read a long time before. "Two of the most important times in a man's life is when he leaves home...and when he returns." I wondered if this anonymous author might also have served in combat somewhere and, fortunately, was able to make it back again for Christmas, too.

I changed my travel itinerary to help a still grieving family cope with their loss, even if my own parents had to wait a few extra days for my return. I'd already been gone a year at war and I realized that *my* home was no longer a world away, merely a short flight hop. The fellow soldier I intended to honor with my presence was an eternity away from his family. This was a fact that was never going to change for them.

Robert Robeson

Robert has had his articles, short stories and poems published 950 times in 330 publications in 130 countries and 73 anthologies. This includes the Reader's Digest, Writer's Digest, Vietnam Combat and Soldier of Fortune, among others. He's a life member of the National Writers Association, VFW, Dustoff Association and the Distinguished Flying Cross Society. He retired as a lieutenant colonel from a 27-year military career as an Army, helicopter medical evacuation pilot on three continents and combat in Vietnam. That is where he flew 987 missions for over 2,500 patients from both sides of the action, had seven aircraft shot up by enemy fire and was shot down twice in one year (1969-1970). He then served as a newspaper managing editor and columnist. He has a BA in English from the University of Maryland—College Park and has completed extensive undergraduate and graduate work in journalism at the University of Nebraska—Lincoln. He lives in Lincoln with his wife, Phyllis, of 54 years. Robert doesn't sport any tattoos and has somehow survived on this planet for 81 years. Though he doesn't fly anymore, he still has a distinct distaste for loud noises and people he doesn't know shooting at him.

Drawknife
By Bill Weatherford

Most boys like their grandfathers. I know I liked mine. He came in handy in the years when my dad and I needed the distance that fathers and sons sometimes need. You can hurt a dad easily, and vice a versa, but a grandfather is tougher to hurt … and vice a versa.

His full name was Fredrick Haarm Telkamp, and he signed his initials with the most beautify penned letters I have ever seen, *F.H.T.*

A hard-working German-American farmer with a wisp of romance and rough arts about him, he made time with me more thoughtfully fun than simply indulgent. I think a clue to our relationship lay in an old ceramic bulldog that sat on a dresser in his farmhouse. The figure's face had been blackened during a fire when grandfather was a young boy, and there was a date of 1883 on its left hind leg. My mother said it was his only toy while growing up, so, perhaps he'd simply been waiting all his life for someone to come out and play.

He had a farm that was a young boy's island for ground-floor fantasy. There were outbuildings to hide in, chickens to scare and roosters who got even. There was the fishpond and a park to fascinate, a ditch to sail and sink boats in, sixty acres of dirt clods to throw, a creepy tank house with an "I dare you to" external staircase. Most of all, there were trees, trees that a boy could never tire of climbing: a lovely fir to hear the wind in, an oak to measure your courage, and a walnut, thick, broad and flat-forked. You could get *shot* out of it by every kind of bad guy and perform tremendous feats of death safely into the soft earth below.

On Saturday nights my parents had a card club in the fall, winter and early spring, before harvest consumed everyone and their time. That meant I was going to spend the weekend with the best friend an only child could have in a country existence. I packed my pajamas for show, knowing I'd sleep in my underwear like he did. I looked forward to getting in bed with him where I could thumb my nose, once and for all, at all the boogiemen who ever lived. His snoring never kept me awake; it just kept them far, far away.

....

I haven't mentioned my grandmother yet. I never learned to love her until later years when one could forgive all the hands she made me wash and rooms I couldn't play in. He loved her though and stopped farming at eighty only because she was so sick that she needed his full-time care.

She was a virtuoso violinist who spoiled her health while studying music at The Julliard School of Music in New York City. To get over T. B. she moved to New Mexico. There, she met my grandfather at his farm while buying apples for a picnic. They courted by carriage, married and soon moved to California's San Joaquin Valley; there she spent most of the rest of her days giving music lessons to the children of farmers and small-town businessmen. It was a long way from anybody's philharmonic.

Ironically, Gramp knew only one piece of music that he would play, always left handed only, on her studio piano: "Oh what a Gal Was Mary." He played it every day before supper, which is rightly called dinner on a farm. He would sing along with a voice that gave him quiet pleasure, and then he would come and eat, no questions asked.

On those Saturday's I would spend with them I would arrive, be overwhelmed by grandmother's blue hair, of course wash my hands and be gladly told to play outside. I'd *mime-kiss* my mother goodbye and then be off to reclaim everything I had missed in a week, working my way out to wherever Gramp was farming. You had to be careful when you came up to him, because he didn't hear well, even in his sixties, as far back as I can remember him. I learned to whistle a tune when I got close so that he could first hear me coming. This was always rewarded by a smile that was so very glad to come out of seclusion, the most gentlemanly smile a man could possibly make.

He would stop his shoveling, or irrigating, or pruning, and, depending upon the season, we started a fire to warm ourselves or ducked under a vineyard trellis to escape the heat. If I came early enough, he'd have saved his midday snack to share. Looking back, he always saved that snack to share, and it was always a crazy combination of what didn't go together but tasted wonderful, just the same. At the house we would have what I would have eaten at home, but he would also give me the only coffee I would ever drink as a child, and, now and then, a taste of Tokay wine from a bottle, at his foot, under the table.

Our talks in the field were more a plan for the evening and Sunday instead of a recap of the week. We always seemed to have a present and a future with no need of the past; my choices were many and his participation guaranteed. Gramps was a sport without the Devil in him: the perfect catalyst, the perfect payer of perfect compliments, the perfect asker of perfect questions, the perfect doer of perfect deeds.

One plan we never discussed until later, however: what we would have for Sunday breakfast. That was saved for the last ritual of the evening. Shirtless, he would wash up again in the bathroom sink, and I'd talk to him as I sat on the tub. I would marvel at the arms on that old man, arms forged by thousands of picks and shovels and pitchforks, thousands of milkings and grain bucking and plowing. He would catch me looking and smile his gentleman's smile, then, earnestly, he'd say something crazy like, "Why did God give men breasts too since we don't need 'em?" I'd just giggle at first, but then I'd have to ponder until bedtime: breasts on men, dang.

Eventually, I'd follow him to the sleeping porch. There he would put on the creams and oils and liniments of age, wind his alarm clock, kiss grandmother in her bed at the other end of the room, sigh, yawn, a throat clearing and finally, *The Question:* "Well, what would you like for breakfast?"

My hemming's and hawing's were about as coded as his, and I wondered if he understood me the way I understood him. Anyway, the answer was always pancakes. He would agree, and the next day I would eat the best pancakes a boy has ever eaten. Always.

After breakfast I would be on my own while he tended to his machinery: to grease, oil, clean for the week. It was my building time, and with grape stakes, wooden raisin trays, lug boxes and scrap I would make the houses and castles of youth. Later, he would always respectfully peruse and improve: a vase of flowers, a rug from the old tenant house or, one time, a kerosene lamp that we'd light, even in the middle of a bright day.

Once, I dug a shallow hole in the side of his main irrigation ditch, and he told me about Carlsbad Caverns, stalactites and stalagmites, and asked me if I wanted some for my cave. He then went into his smokehouse and came back with about a dozen turnips that he stuck in the roof and floor of the hole.

Stepping back he admired his work for a moment, and then began to chuckle in his slow, gently rolling way. He said that was the first good use he ever made of a turnip, that usually they just made him burp. Then he was off to change the oil in his old Case tractor, and I was left to giggle and ponder turnips and burping until I finally *blew up* my cave, stalactites, stalagmites and all. Oh, yes, the days of blowing things up.

....

It was my penchant for *making* and his encouragement to do so that finally brought about a tree house. At some point in life, he had also been a cabinetmaker, and much of their house, finish work and all, had been from his own hands and tools. They were artisan's tool, old and archaic-looking in comparison to my father's, but if it was a chisel, it was sharp, a plane, it was true, a hammer…it belonged to your hand.

My favorite tool was the drawknife, a shaping tool that you pulled towards you with both hands. There were no guides to a drawknife save your own sense and what he would call, *The Feel*. I had rarely seen anyone else ever use one, let alone as fast and perfectly as the work that fell from his.

One Saturday afternoon, sitting in the water grass of an irrigation flat-furrow, I broached the subject of building a tree house, and what did he think of the matter? He chewed thoughtfully about two and a half graham crackers worth and answered that it wasn't a bad idea. Then he mused through a piece of Spam and asked me if I had a tree in mind. I told him, probably a walnut because they forked low, were sturdy and would be the easiest to work in. We both drank warm tap water from a Mason jar and then went looking for a tree.

Out back of his work yard, where his old barn had stood in the days he farmed with mules and Percheron horses, was the biggest English walnut on the ranch. We walked around it, agreed that it was a worthy tree and went to the tool shed for some butcher paper and a plan.

It had been my habit when working in that shed, in more unsophisticated years, to just start hammering, sawing and whittling until, whatever you had, would start to look like something; then, you'd finish making whatever that was. I have since learned that it was more acceptable to have a plan, and, if I ever wanted to learn the feel of a drawknife, I would do whatever it took, be it making plans, eating Spam or playing songs, left-handed only, on the piano.

We looked at the lumber we had in the woodpile; we looked at the structure of the tree. On paper, we decided on a triangular floor frame, a half wall railing, a ladder going up along with a rope swing and an upper lookout deck like a ship's; we were both enamored of the sea. The rest of the late afternoon, we pulled out stock, measured it and put it aside for the next day. Tools were set out too, some at age ten, I had never used before: a spirit level, a plumb line and a chalk box.

We played cribbage that night as usual, got ready for bed our same ways and placed the anticipated order for pancakes in the morning. We both slept well, me dreaming of tree houses, safely surrounded by warm snoring.

That Sunday's breakfast was one of the biggest and best I ever ate. There was no hurrying, no rush; one can't if you want to do things right, and a tree house, especially your first, simply can't be done any other way. Finally, we went to the shed and took our tools to the site. The material had been carried down in the dusk of the evening before, after dinner. We looked at our plan; we looked at our tools; we went to work.

…

I remember little of the job as a whole; I do remember it was hard for grandfather to have to hang off the ladder sometimes, and I remember we used zinc nails because they were also good for the tree. The spirit level was fun to use, and I got to take charge of it, not just to hold it like I would have at home. I was the one who *read it*, and I was to live with what I read.

I have no idea how long it took to finish. It wasn't like it was a dream or anything; it wasn't like it got done on its own. It was just a total flowing pleasure of doing, of being equal, of being together in silence until words were needed to be together in task. It must be the same feeling an old man and woman have after loving each other for many years, after they have gotten to the point when they almost look alike, when age isn't grotesque or ugly, but full in an understanding anticipation that not everyone gets to achieve.

Sometime in the afternoon it was done. We stepped back to look at it; we got in it to look again; we decided it was "O.K. Jake,". I'd learned "O.K., Jake" was old *muleskinner talk*. It meant, "pretty goddamned good," but you could use it in front of ladies and parents because they didn't know what it meant.

Anyway, when you have a tree house that is "O.K., Jake," it's time to put away the tools, which we did. Then, Gramp went to catch up on his machinery for the week, and I went to personalizing my tree house.

...

Over the next three years that place became more sacred than my room at home. Not because you didn't have to clean it, because I kept it immaculate, but because it was truly an extension of my own hands and the perfection of it: the food stores, the roof, the phone I built from a Cub Scout book, the telescope, the weapons: catapults and crossbows. I even had a bucket with carefully punched holes in the bottom and ran a hose up to it for a shower. I only used it once, and it worked. I probably would have tried it again if my first experience hadn't been in February. Still, it really looked great if all it did was just hang there. It was grandfather, though, who really came up with the crowning compliment to that wonderful, wonderful place; he had it insured.

When Mr. Ralph Carlisle, the local agent, came out to renew my grandfather's current polices, Gramp said that, in the interests of my investment of time, effort and material, it should have fire, theft and liability protection of which he then bought two dollars and fifty cents worth. I felt like such a man of property, that I invited Mr. Carlisle's son, Sherpi, who was the closest thing our town could boast of a village idiot, to accompany me and have a look. Knowing better now, I assume he had a form of autism. His *difference* today would have a better understanding and thoughtfulness, perhaps, something we'll never know. Anyway, he came with his father, and I was just sort of proud that, at almost thirty, he got pretty excited as we walked out to the tree house.

Sherpi always talked really fast and mostly about sports. On Sundays, he'd read the Green Sheet in church, not like he was a hypocrite either. He didn't hide it but held it up in front of God and everyone and would even rattle it out smooth if it got wrinkled, sometimes right in the middle of silent prayer. Well, he might have known about every sport and every athlete and every statistic in the world and talked so fast nobody could understand, but he surely didn't know a thing about tree houses. He smacked his head going up, missed a rung on the way to the lookout, and I brought him down before he became my first liability.

...

My grandfather's gift would become a wonderful childhood bookmark. Most of the memories were solitary or included him only in the original partnership. There was one, however, that marked, in a very small way, a coming of age; it was a dirt clod fight I got into with Dwight Bachman. He and I were to take part in a late spring music recital in my grandmother's parlor. Now this should have been a real treat because that was about the only time I had ever been allowed inside the parlor; the performance piano was there so it couldn't be helped.

At 2:00 we were to start off the show, Dwight on the piano with something that sounded pretty good to me, and I was to follow with the most simplified and mercifully short version of "Clair de Lune" on the violin. It still wasn't simple or short enough to cover the fact that my heart or any other part of me would never master the violin. When you know that at eleven, you know it for life, so, at 1:30, we slipped out into the San Joaquin Valley heat in our white shirts and black bow ties. With me in the high ground of my carefully outfitted fortress, but he with the mobility of the open ground, we traded clod splotches on our *whiteness* made worse by the sweat that steamed through from underneath.

Grandfather was the one who caught us. We were in so much trouble. Still, the clod fight had been a choice we made, and in a way, so was my destruction of "Clair de Lune", especially with a music-teaching grandmother who had ruined her health at Julliard. Gramp was the only one who truly understood my rebellion though he never said a word; he loved her and me both.

...

By age thirteen I was in high school, and things began to change and run together. Now I didn't stay with my grandparents much on weekends. I had activities, games to play in and started doing our own farm work with my father. At fifteen, sixteen and seventeen I was trading what we all trade as we grow up… what we can trust and count on, for things we know nothing about, at a pace we don't need, but are absolutely certain we just have to have or do them.

Later, it was away to college and what happens to you there. When I was a junior, I came home in January because grandmother had died, not unexpectedly. Grandfather had become very shrunken, and his arms were no longer a marvel. He had sold his farm and taken her to Fresno where she was closer to the doctor as she neared the end of life. I had gotten to know and like her a lot in those years; I washed my hands on my own then, and she let her blue hair go a lovely white.

At her funeral, I remember him crying and taking people up to the casket saying, "Come see what's left of us, come see what's left." He was weeping. I'd never seen him cry; I'd never seen my father cry; I couldn't even remember myself crying, not since I put my upper tooth through my lower lip with a pogo stick at twelve. Anyway, I couldn't cry at the funeral; I couldn't even cry for him. I felt awful that I couldn't, but I couldn't even cry about that.

Afterwards he lived alone for many years. I married, had children, got divorced, and then married again. I would go visit him from time to time, and he would be good company. We'd talk like the old days, of the present and the future, very little of the past, except at things like the moon walk. He would recount that he had been twenty years old when the Wright brothers flew the first plane, or about the draft and how he'd been thirty-four and too old for it in World War I.

Now he is ninety-nine; he lives half each year with my mom and dad and the other half with my aunt. His health isn't strong but he's still surprising at times and not senile. Sometimes, his poor hearing walls him off, but it's hardest to watch his lack of something to do and to be. He once told me, "Dean isn't it odd that when you're young you have so much to do that you don't have time to sleep, but when you're old, you don't need any sleep, and you don't have anything to do?"

I see him sit sometimes and look out the windows at a snowfall, or watch the twinkle lights on the Christmas tree all day long. What are you thinking grandfather? Do I ever dare to ask you? Do you remember the snacks we ate together? What are the words to, "Oh What a Gal Was Mary?" Can you still taste the pancakes like I can? Do you know what you have taught me and how plentiful all of it is? I can weep now and say, "Come see what is left of us", and I've learned never to work without a plan. I always insure my tree houses, and the feel of the drawknife, though illusive, is being worked on in the years of not enough sleep. I wish you could come out and play grandfather; I wish you could come out and play.

Bill Weatherford

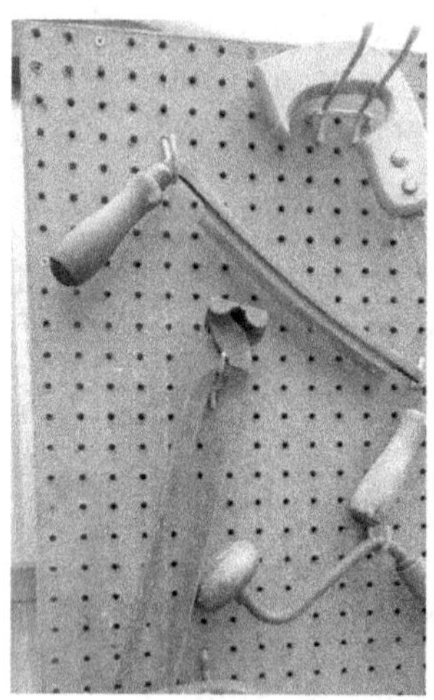

Bill Weatherford is a native Californian. He grew up in a small San Joaquin Valley town and much of his writing has its roots in the central part of the state. Having a farmer father who self-described as a former "football bum", and a ballerina for a mom, Bill had a wide range of gods to please…and to learn from. He completed his undergrad and graduate work at UC Berkeley but returned to the San Joaquin. There it became a passion to promote the virtues and opportunities, the kindnesses, and fullness of a place that feeds much of the world but often gets little respect. We have wonderful art, music, history, multicultural splendor; children of 79 languages go to our schools. All that means, we have some special stories and Bill tries to tell a few.

Primarily a short story writer, he also wrote the screenplay, produced and directed the 2014 feature film, *Underclassmen*. He hopes to produce another of his screenplays, *Killing Flies*. At present, Bill is looking to publish a first novel, *Tilly&Turp*, a book that starts out like a YA but finds richness and power from a 12-year-old girl whose first words about Fresno were, "Are we on earth?"

The Faller
By Brad Bennett

John studied the French countryside. It appeared safe enough...lots of open country spread across wide grass fields. In the distance, he could see a wooded area, but that was good, too far away for a sniper. The dirt roadway was rough, bouncing him around in the back of the small truck like a toy doll. The vehicle's wooden bench was hard on his ass. But it was a lot harder for the five captured German soldiers crammed in with him. They could barely move...packed together with their hands tightly bound.

John reached into his shirt pocket and pulled out a cigarette. He lit it and took a deep breath. He noticed the young soldier beside him was watching.

"Bitte?" the young German asked, motioning to his mouth.

John smiled. "Sure." He placed the cigarette in the soldier's clasped hands.

"Danke," the soldier said. He took a deep drag, smiled, and handed the cigarette back.

John nodded, "Danke."

Suddenly came a far-off roaring noise...getting louder! John glanced down the long roadway. Circling fast was a yellow-nosed fighter plane turning to make a run at them! He jumped up and pounded hard on the roof of the cab. "MESSERSCHMITT! Stop the truck! Get out! Get out!"

The driver slammed on the brakes and skidded to a stop.

"Raus! Raus!" John yelled to the prisoners. The men quickly jumped, more accurately fell, out of the back of the truck.

The aircraft was almost upon them, its engine screaming. John helped those who were stumbling and guided them to the safety of the ditch. The fighter's twin cannons opened up with a deafening staccato of bullets, stitching down the roadway until they hit the truck, ripping the back to pieces. The fighter disappeared in the distance, but everyone stayed hidden, afraid the menace might return. Finally, after ten minutes, the driver, and the Lieutenant riding with him, popped back up. The officer motioned for John to regroup the prisoners. The hands-bound Germans were scattered up and down the embankment. Suddenly one of them jumped from the roadway and began running for the far-off woods. "HALT!" John yelled, running forward. Then the other prisoners jumped from the roadway and also began sprinting across the field.

"Shoot them, Corporal, screamed the officer." Don't let them get away!"

John raised his rifle, then hesitated. "I can't shoot tied prisoners!" He yelled back.

The Lieutenant was furious. "GOD DAMN IT, SHOOT THEM! That's an order!" The officer yanked out his pistol and began firing, but the small weapon was no good for the distant moving targets.

John tucked his M1 Garand under his chin, took aim, and fired. The farthest man away fell. He aimed at the next man. "Halt. Halt!" He yelled out, but the man kept going." He fired again...the second farthest man fell. John tried wounding the next man, aiming for his shoulder. The runner faltered, then kept on. John crammed in another ammo clip, his voice screaming, "HALT, HALT!" repeatedly firing until all four runners were down.

The Lieutenant came forward. "There's one going in the woods!" he yelled, pointing to the trees.

John started running across the field to where the wounded German had entered the forest. The man's trail of blood was a giveaway. John tracked him through the foliage and found him lying on his back, his chest gurgling with a deep rasp. He had been shot through the lungs. The soldier raised his hand, blood spitting from his mouth. He was horribly wounded. "Kill mien!" he pleaded in broken English. John raised his rifle.

The two men standing back at the truck heard the rifle crack. They winced. All the soldiers were down now. The air smelled of gunpowder and death.

On returning to the bullet-ridden vehicle, John recognized the prisoner he had given the smoke to. He checked for the fallen man's breathing. He was dead. John took the soldier's tags and walked back to the truck. The Lieutenant approached him. "Are you Ok?" He asked.

John didn't answer. He went to the roadside, and sat

silently, with head in his hands.

***

After the war in 1947, John Schindler met Janine Bennett. She was hitchhiking to the little burg of Monmouth in the Willamette Valley. She heard there was a waitress job there, but she had no car, so she walked. John saw her, hit the brakes, and immediately stopped. It was a no-brainer, pretty young girl, good-looking young vet. They immediately hit it off, and it was only a short time before they married.

But there was a snag. Janine was recently divorced with a four-year-old son. That would be me. My nickname was Sonny.

John worked as a faller, the elite of the loggers. Fallers had the highest-paying job of all the forest workers up and down the Pacific coast. His job was to bring down the giant Douglas firs that towered over the land. However, he would also be the first to be laid off after the big trees were cut. Then he had to move on and find a new hiring site. But the job did have an upside, it allowed him a lot of free time at home between jobs.

Over time, the young married couple produced two

more children, Johnny, Jr., and Mary Ann. However, Janine still worked, and looking after three kids soon proved a problem, my presence wasn't sitting well with John.

As I grew older, it was decided it was best if I stayed with John's widowed mother on her farm in the Willamette valley. She was living alone and gladly took me in. Occasionally John and Janine would visit and leave the other kids there too. Over time, John was beginning to subject me to harsh treatment whenever he came by. He was tough on his own kids, but for some reason, he singled me out. His personality could change to a meanness that was scary. I became wary of him and kept my distance whenever he was around. Of course, it didn't help when he drank. Then he could be terrifying. Once, he found me playing near the house. He came over and started a verbal assault, railing at me for being weak and worthless. He threatened me and told me he'd take me out and dump me somewhere on the side of the road, like the many stray dogs that wandered onto the farm. But then, inexplicably, he would be friendly the next time he came. Then just as quickly, he'd go back on the attack.

It was scary as hell. He was a big lumberjack, bull strong from carrying a heavy saw in the woods. But I was never afraid he would physically hurt me. It was always verbal.

Then one day in mid-summer, when I was about thirteen, he did something unimaginable. I remember he drove up in the yard, opened the car trunk, and motioned for me to come over. He pulled out a small shotgun and handed it to me. "It's yours," he said. "I want you to have it."

This sudden change was unreal. Even more so was why? Why now? Maybe he realized I was growing up, I had no real father, so perhaps he judged I was ready. He was going to train me to be a hunter like him.

John's favorite pastime was hunting for pheasants in the high, open fields beyond the farm, and there were plenty of them in the myriad of fencerows that surrounded the area. "We'll go out this Saturday," John said, "and get us a rooster."

So that would be the day I went hunting with my stepfather. We were up early that morning and started through the woodland behind the house. There was a little trail winding up the hill where I often played. But now I was a real hunter with a real gun, not a boy with a toy, and even better, I was with him like his real son.

We started into the forest, and I trailed behind him carrying the shotgun. This area I loved, and it had special meaning for me. Once, it was my fantasy place. But now I was growing up, and I must put those childish things away. Then came an event I will never forget, a tree limb was blocking part of the trail. John turned to push it aside, and at that exact moment, he saw me holding the shotgun, I had accidentally pointed it at him. He whirled and swatted the gun back.

"God Dammit, Sonny!" he snapped at me. "Don't EVER point a gun at a man!"

I pulled back in fear. "I'm sorry, I forgot."

"You hold that gun straight up. You hear me?" John's voice was stern. His sudden change was frightening. "Do you know what it's like to shoot a man?" He asked as if I might. "You pay attention."

As we walked on, I realized I had been charged with serious responsibility. Before, I had carried the gun happily. Now, it had become an awful burden, and I tried to think of nothing else but the position of the barrel.

Soon we reached the end of the woods, where the trail led down into a little ravine, then back up to an old wire fence that skirted the fields. I followed him down, picking my footing carefully. I had come through here many times, but not toting a shotgun. John bounded the fence effortlessly and stood studying the open field. I struggled with the wire, trying to steady the gun, then my hand slipped off the stock. I attempted to re-grab it, but it came up and pointed at John. At that precise moment, he turned and saw the barrel.

"YOU GODDAM STUPID ASS!" He shouted at me. The words exploded out, ringing my ears. John rushed forward and snatched the shotgun from my grasp.

"DAMN, your stupid ass!" He shouted again. He yanked open the gun chamber, ejecting the shell to the ground. "SEE THAT!" he railed at me, pointing at the shell. "That can take a man's head off. You don't listen, do you? You're too goddamn stupid. Well, you won't last long as a hunter." John's tirade was relentless. I stood trembling in silence. John's explosive words seemed to be absorbed by the nearby fir trees, almost as if they were listening...standing like a silent crowd of gathered witnesses to my humiliation. "I knew a kid in the army who was thick-headed like you!" He railed on. "He got blown to bits the first day we hit the beach!" John picked up the shell and crammed it back into the breach. "You're a bastard child. Do you know that? Your father, whoever he is, is probably dead. And that's how you'll wind up if you don't start listening."

He shouldered the shotgun, grabbed me, and shoved me forward. "Get moving, goddamn you. I'll carry the gun."

My hands were shaking. I wouldn't cry, I told myself. I wouldn't let the man see me cry. Suddenly a shrieking pheasant exploded from the fencerow. John brought the gun smoothly to his shoulder, traced the bird's flight, and fired. The bird fell like a stone.

"Go get it!" he barked.

I ran over to the dying pheasant; the smell of gunpowder filled the air. The bird flopped about the yellow grain stubble, speckling it crimson red.

"Pick it up," John shouted.

I grabbed the bird's throbbing legs and hurried back to John, holding it away from my body as I ran. The bird stubbornly clung to life, flopping and quivering.

"Wring its neck." He snapped. I hesitated, staring helplessly at the bird.

"You're a goddamned sissy, aren't you?" He grabbed the pheasant and twirled it around by its head. The bird squawked and died.

We continued onward across the field. I trailed behind him with the dead pheasant. It was appropriate I carried the bird. We were comrades in disgrace. Only the bird would not know any disfavor. It was dead. I, however, would have to live on with my shame. As we marched on, I stared up at the big man's back, his ugly words rolling over and over in my mind. Finally, I could bear no more. I dropped the bird and ran past him. On across the field I ran until I reached the woods. I clambered over the fence and rushed headlong down the trail. I didn't dare look back. Surely The Hunter could easily catch me. I charged along the winding path, brush swatting my face. I caught my foot on a tree root and sprawled face down in the dirt, bloodying my nose. I got up and ran on. Finally, I reached the safety of the house. I sat on the back porch to catch my breath. There was nowhere else I could go. I waited for another verbal assault upon his arrival. But when John reached the house, he grabbed a beer from the fridge, went to his car, and drove away. I sat there, both terrified and confused.

Strangely, John's abuse eased back in the next few days, but I still avoided him. It was as if some antithesis had transformed him, and he was now unburdened. It was bizarre. I never told my mother what happened that day. Not then, not ever.

As the years passed, and I grew older and saw less of John, he and my mother had finally divorced. His drinking and her fighting with him had finally taken their toll. Then one day, when I was in my mid-teens, my mother came by the farm and told me to pack my things. I, and the other children were going to live with her, and her new husband Bob.

His name was Robert Murphy. He owned a large ranch in northeast Oregon and treated me well. He put me to work riding horses on his spread, herding cattle. Soon I became a free-range cowboy, and I enjoyed my new life. But after high school, I decided I wanted to see the rest of the world. I talked to Bob about my plans and he mentioned the military. He had no college, but the Army Air Force needed pilots and they provided him with pilot training. After the war, he returned to ranching, but he kept an old Beechcraft for pleasure flying.

In 1963, I took Bob's advice and joined the Us Air Force. My mother then drove me to the recruiting station in Portland. From there, I would leave for Texas by train to start my basic training at Lackland Air Force base. After signing all the papers, we sat in the waiting area expecting my approval, but then an officer came out and summoned me privately. I left my mother sitting there with a look of panic on her face. I wondered what was going on. Once in the man's office, he shut the door.

"Son," he said, "your name, Brad Schindler, doesn't exist. Instead, we found your birth certificate, your real name is Brad Bennett."

Now I was both hurt and angry. I came out and confronted my grief-stricken mother, whose secret was now exposed. Then she confessed it all to me.

"I'm so sorry Brad, but Bennett, my first husband, wasn't your father either. You were born out of wedlock by a Merchant Sailor I met before I married."

Now everything was explained. In the 1950s, a mother with a bastard child was an outcast. I had grown up and gone through high school with a false name. That night, I boarded the train for basic training in Texas, angry and disillusioned. I vowed never to live in Oregon again. I would only return periodically to visit.

***

We were all standing in the Air Force Base parking lot in San Antonio, Texas. I was in a group of recruits, we had just arrived on a bus, and now we were about to get our first taste of boot camp by a drill instructor, or DI. He ordered us into a ragtag line and began calling roll.

"Brad Bennett." The instructor barked out when he got to my name.

I stood silent.

"BRAD BENNETT!" He shouted.

I suddenly realized that it was me. "Here!" I yelled out.

"You dumb ass!" He yelled in my face. "Don't you know your name?"

"No, sir, I don't!" (*Best I stop here and not list the litany of 4-letter words that emanated from that man's mouth.)*

After finishing boot camp, I went in for my assignment interview. In high school I had received good marks in art and writing, sadly, not much in anything else. But fortunately, the Air Force needed artists for Aircraft Maintenance illustrations, and thanks to my school record, I qualified. I then began training as a Technical Illustrator. This gave me the start of my career later as a graphic designer. Thank God I had listened to Bob.

After leaving the Air Force, I moved to Dallas and found work as an artist doing graphic Illustration. It had been a long time since I visited Oregon, except for a few short trips to see my mother, who had divorced Bob. They had started fighting, and sadly, Bob then turned to drink. He later died in the drunk tank in Vancouver Washington.

It was during this time I also learned that Johnny Jr. had disappeared. It was suspected he was mixed up with some drug dealers, and they did him in. Johnny's body has never been found. A few years later, Mary Ann died after a long life of drug addiction. She had been a user since high school. So sad, they both had so much promise.

***

Years later, in the late seventies, I received a call from my Aunt Alicia. Would I come up for a visit? I liked my aunt because she often visited me as a child. Her life had been successful, and she always helped out with other family members when needed. So, I took some time off and flew up to Salem for a short visit. Unfortunately, my girlfriend Jan couldn't get off work, so I came alone.

Oregon's Willamette Valley in late August is special, like it always was when I stayed here as a boy. Now, I stood, gazing across the waving grain where I often played when my mother had left me here during the summers. As a grown man, I still felt the urge to run across this field, climb one of the old apple trees down by the pond, and sit up among the branches, eating the tangy wild fruit.

"Still peaceful here, isn't it?" Alicia said, "I always love coming here to visit."

"Did you think of selling it after your mother died?"

"Oh, not then, but I'm getting on now, and it's a chore

to look after it."

"I appreciate you bringing me by here Alicia. I wish I could have had Jan up from Texas with me, but maybe next time."

"Well thank you for coming, Brad, and yes, please do."

"For sure," I said as we began walking back to the car.

That night after dinner, Alicia updated me on the family happenings over a few glasses of chardonnay. I listened attentively, and then Alicia mentioned that John was staying close by. Alicia was John's younger sister.

"John's here," I said, somewhat nervous. "Here in Salem?"

"Yes, I've been looking after him since he was badly injured in the woods. I've found him a place nearby to stay with help from the local VFW."

"You know Alicia," I said, trying not to be too condemning, "that man gave me nothing but sheer hell when I was a kid, so I must be honest. I'm sorry, but I hated that man.

Alicia set her glass down, and leaned forward. "Brad, before John left for that damn war, he was the best brother a sister could ask for. But when he returned from overseas, his up-and-down personality was hard to deal with. But we had to put up with him because we were sworn to a family secret by my mother."

This was a shocker. "What secret?"

"We learned after the war that John was being held at Walter Reed Veterans Hospital in Bethesda, Maryland, for observation. They informed our mother that he wasn't physically wounded, but he was there for medical evaluation, which suggested John was suffering from severe mental stress. He didn't come home until months later."

"I never heard that."

"Yes, back then they knew very little about mental illness, and mother didn't want John to be seen as a coward. But of course we all knew he wasn't. John was among the first to land at Normandy beach. He fought across France, a decorated war hero."

"My God, Alicia, that explains it all," I said. "So he lived with that all this time.

"Yes, only his brother and I knew about it." She looked at me with a somewhat pleading face. "Brad, would you like to visit John now? You will find him to be a different man. He talks about you often."

This was a surprise. I was nervous as hell, but now I felt I should see him. "Yes, Alicia, I'll do it." I said with a somewhat mixed emotion.

The next day Alicia gave me her car keys and John's location, a one-room flat in a motel on the outskirts of the city. She explained how to get there, then I left and proceeded to the address. As I drove, I tried to work on my greeting line. But I couldn't think of what to say. I couldn't imagine him any different from the man I knew.

I soon found the motel, parked, got out, and searched for his apartment, anxiety building in my gut with each step. I located his door, knocked, and waited. I heard a creaking noise, a shuffling sound from inside, then finally, the door opened.

Standing in the doorway was a frail, weak older man I barely recognized. When he saw me, his face lit up, and his eyes widened. He was so delighted I thought he would cry. "Sonny!" he said. "It is so good to see you," he gave me his hand.

I had no words how to answer. Whatever I was going

to say evaporated. I took his hand, "hello John," I said, "It's good to see you too."

"Come on in Son," then he held his arm to me. "Can you help me a bit? I'm afraid it's hard for me to get around." He motioned to his walker by the door, I turned it around so he could use it to go back. "How have you been, Sonny? Alicia told me you might visit me someday. I am so happy you did. Have a seat and tell me what you've been doing?"

My mind was spinning. I didn't know what to say, so I started yammering about my life to date. He acted attentive, but it was apparent he had trouble focusing. Finally, I dared to ask him what had happened out in those woods.

"Oh, God," he said. "This jackass newbie fell a tree on me while I sat on a stump eating my lunch. They fired the son of a bitch, but it sure ended my career. Now I'm on a pension. My nephew visited once, but he doesn't come around anymore. So I'm mostly alone here."

As we sat and talked, I kept asking myself, who was this gentle old fellow before me? Then, I noticed he still had that same jocular, goofy laugh that amused me as a boy. Yes, I still knew him, that part remained.

When it came time for me to leave, John had one last request. "Could you fix my bed son? A slat has fallen out, and it's damn uncomfortable to lie on."

"Of course," I answered. I slid under the bed and adjusted the slat. When I came back out, I noticed other things amiss in the room. His small TV was placed awkwardly, making it difficult for him to watch. I rearranged his furniture and put it nearer his bed. I looked around the room for more deeds to do. My lifetime of hatred had now evaporated. My self-pity now became a slap in my face. I felt foolish. Here was this poor man, suffering and abandoned, and all I had on my mind was hatred and revenge, revenge for what? What a waste of emotion I had placed upon myself.

Finally, when it was time to go, I shook John's hand warmly this time. This was a self-realizing experience. I now felt nothing but empathy for this man. I had spent my whole life hating him, but why? What had made him what he was?

At the door, I retook his hand. "I will try to return and see you again, John, I promise."

"Thank you so much, Sonny," he said. "Please come back. I would like that."

Sadly, I couldn't return to Oregon that year because of a busy workload. Then towards the year's end, Alicia called me and said he had died.

****

Years later, after John had passed, I learned some of John's war story in France. It came from a distant cousin, who had learned it from his father before him. This story finally filled in the last chapter of John's history. Now I could reason why he reacted so accusingly on that day he took me hunting. My pointing that gun barrel at him gave a visual image of HIS gun firing at those fleeing prisoners. He saw those bullets ripping through their hand-tied bodies. He was the one pulling the trigger. He lived the rest of his life trying to forget that day in France. Maybe he could let it go for a while, but it must have always returned with a flash of memory. And when it did, he shifted it away, on me, or anyone else. I was merely around more often.

Of course, a psychologist could read John's history and provide a better answer. But I can say that when I visited him that day, it was evident his dementia had taken most of it away. In some ways, that was a blessing. His horrible memories were now erased. What I saw was a man finally freed from his past.

The irony is, I was freed as well.

Brad Bennett

Brad now lives with his wife, Norrie, in Oliver BC, "Canada's Wine Capital," in the heart of the Okanagan Valley. Since both retiring, they have enjoyed the beauty of this land, and frequently have their grandchildren up from the Vancouver coast for visits. Norrie loves visiting all the grape wineries here, and some are Canada's best. Alas, Brad can't drink wine, he's allergic to sulphites "I didn't like the damn stuff anyway," Brad says, "just give me a good dark ale."

Brad was born in Oregon, and grew up in the Willamette Valley. After a stent as a graphic designer doing flight safety cartoons for the Air Force, Brad moved to Canada and opened a small art studio in Vancouver. There he took up Advertising logo design. Later, as a writer, Brad ventured into TV ads—it was a living, he says, but Brad always wanted to write fiction. So on retirement he has written three books of short stories.

This story featured here is his only nonfiction. It's a story that was very hard to put on paper, Brad says, but now, thanks to Stories through ages, it's finally out.

The Good Things Consignment Shop
By Jeannette M. Bond

Lynn and Joe Miller had owned the Good Things Consignment Shop for about fifteen years, about as long as anyone in Highland could remember. They bought it when Lynn retired from teaching math in the local high school and a couple of years before Joe transferred his accounting business to his nephew. The building was an old Victorian house, with a wrap-around porch, numerous small rooms on the first floor, hallways leading to who knew where and a second floor accessed by a creaky, narrow set of stairs with only a partial handrail. The second floor held mostly clothes, while jewelry, furniture, and electronics were downstairs. Out back was an assortment of garden supplies, lawn furniture and tools.

At prom time and Halloween, a steady stream of kids headed to the second floor for their costumes. In between it attracted a regular set of bargain shoppers, seniors on fixed incomes, people on welfare, college kids or people just getting started. Lynn referred to these as the Shoppers. She prided herself on the quality of the clothes; wool suits, and cashmere sweaters, not polyester and acrylic. The prices were higher than the thrift stores over by the highway, but they were still reasonable for her clientele.

The place was a dilapidated, dusty mess when Lynn and Joe bought it. They could easily have tossed the entire contents, and did toss a lot, but they felt the house had good bones. They figured they would change the standards of what they would accept, to up the exclusivity factor. This formula had worked well over the years. Now Good Things was the first place most people thought about when they thought of buying anything second hand.

During the Fall when the Town of Highland held all these festivals to try to bring in tourists, Lynn knew that most of the customers would be Browsers. She was not particularly interested in them. They came to shops like hers as a pastime, strolled through and maybe occasionally bought something, a Santa, a little knickknack or a lamp. They never went to the second floor or the back yard. They were not true shoppers.

Outside of festival time were those she thought of as People on a Mission. They wanted a specific thing, like throw pillows for a leather couch, and would hit every shop in town on a Saturday morning looking for the perfect find. They never spent more than about five minutes in any shop. These people did not really interest her either. She would help where she could, but was not surprised or concerned when they left after a few minutes.

There were, however, two classes of customers who interested her. The first were the people just starting out, college students, newlyweds, new arrivals to town, the Newbies. They tended to be very careful shoppers and very enthusiastic when they found something they needed. She knew they could be repeat customers if they found Good Things to be helpful and accommodating. For them she was always willing to find a free truck delivery service for any furniture purchases.

The second was a subset of consignors. Many of the people coming in to sell family possessions seemed to have no discernible connection to the family or the goods.

They just wanted to get them off their hands. But a subset, she called the Grieving, were unhappy to be there, sorry to be selling what they considered family heirlooms. Most were not there of their own accord. She watched out for them.

Lynn could be found nearly every day at the front counter, or somewhere on the first floor, sorting and rearranging merchandise. She kept track each day of who came into Good Things in a ledger book she kept under the register. She tallied up the numbers, by categories, as the day went on and made note of the local conditions such as weather, festivals and holidays. Joe, a couple years older than Lynn, took care of almost everything else. He was rarely seen by the customers. He kept to a backroom behind the register and did the bookkeeping, made minor furniture repairs, checked whether appliances worked and even did some jewelry work. Periodically they decided together that there were too many items in the shop and that it was time for a big sale or a big give-away. Lynn assumed one would be coming up in another month or so.

It was late afternoon on a Wednesday in mid-

September when the young man came into the shop. There were no other customers. Lynn did not recognize him as a local. He was tall with pale skin and dark hair. Lynn figured he was in his mid-twenties, maybe he was a Newbie. He headed for the jewelry case. "Let me know if you want to see something and I will open that for you," she said. She returned to today's project of sorting out a new consignment of gold watches.

"I'd like to look at a couple of these rings," he said, a few minutes later.

Lynn made her way to the glass jewelry case and pulled a tray of rings onto the top. "Something special?" she asked.

The young man blushed slightly. "Maybe."

"Does she like vintage pieces or something more contemporary?" asked Lynn, pointing in turn to two rings, as examples.

He paused. "I am not sure," he replied, "but I like this one." He held up a square cut medium diamond in a filigree white gold setting.

"That is a lovely piece that was very popular in the 1920s."

He turned over the tag to look at the price. "I can do that," he said. "What size is that?"

She pulled out a ring sizer gauge. "It is a five. Do you know what size she is?" He shook his head. "Do you want her to come in and try it on?"

"No, I want this to be a surprise," he said with a smile.

"Okay, my husband may be able to adjust the size a bit, otherwise I would recommend Harkins Jewelers over by the Post Office. They are very reasonable."

Lynn took the ring from him, found a ring box under the counter and walked over to the register. She took his credit card, "Daniel Taylor," she noted. "Are you new around here? I don't think I have seen you before."

"I've been here about a month. I'm a new science teacher at the High School."

"Oh, I taught math there for many years before I retired. It was a great place," Lynn replied.

"So far, so good," Dan said, "but it's only been a couple weeks. I am still getting used to things."

Lynn handed him his bag and receipt and watched him leave. Joe poked his head out the door to the backroom. "What was that?"

"A new science teacher at the school, buying an engagement ring. But I have some misgivings for him. He didn't know what style she might like and wanted it to be a surprise." Lynn shook her head.

Joe chuckled. "There you go being a mom again. You would think you'd have had enough of that by now." Together they raised four kids who were scattered all around the country.

"I think it's just instinct at this point," she replied.

A few days later in the mid-morning an older man pulled his late model station wagon to the curb and unloaded a box. He carefully brought it to the door, which Lynn held open. "I have a china set I need to sell," he said.

Lynn figured he was in his early 80s. "Sure, let's see what you have." She opened the box and carefully unwrapped a serving bowl, white porcelain rimmed with pink roses. She turned it over to see the name on the bottom. "This is very nice." She unwrapped a second piece.

"I know," he said, "I hate to be selling this set. It's a

service for 12 with all the side dishes. The rest of the boxes are in the car. My wife and I bought it about 50 years ago in an antique store on the East Coast. We used it for every special dinner. This is just heart-breaking to me." Lynn turned her head slightly as he wiped a tear from his cheek. "She passed on about 9 months ago, heart problems. Now my boys are after me to move into some damn assisted living place and to get rid of everything. And these kids don't want our stuff. Just sell it, they say. Downsize! It is just so sad; they don't appreciate anything."

Lynn nodded. "I hear that a lot. We'll try to find a good home for it." Joe emerged from the back to help the man with the rest of the boxes. "Let me get your information. Name and address?"

"Robert Duncan. I guess you should use that Creekside Manor place in Silvercreek for the address. That's where I will be in another week or so." He shook his head.

"Oh, I know that place. A friend of mine, Anna, moved in there a year or so ago. She likes it. She says there is lots to do, even fishing, she likes to fish." Lynn smiled at him. "I bet you settle right in."

"I doubt it," he replied morosely. "Let me give you my son Steve's information, too. He is here in town."

They finished the consignment paperwork. "Do you have any idea what price you want? We take a 30% commission."

Robert shrugged. "I'm not in it for the money."

"I'm thinking $300, but let me take a look at the other sets we have to see how they are priced."

"That's fine," he remarked as he turned to leave. He stopped at the door. "Don't be surprised if my boys come in shortly with the rest of my belongings."

Joe came out from the backroom. "More china, huh? These sets are hard to get rid of. And I heard that mention of your friend Anna. Are you back to meddling in matchmaking?"

"Me? Never!" Lynn made a mental note to give Anna a call.

The Duncan china set did not sit long. A middle-aged Couple on a Mission picked it up less than a week later. Maybe I set the price too low at $350, Lynn thought, as she watched the couple pack the boxes into a small sports car. But they seemed very happy to get it.

"I have an idea for a Fall Sale, said Lynn to Joe one evening when they were closing. Let's do an auction, with a real auctioneer. I bet we could get a lot of people out for it. It would be an event. Let's do it on a Saturday, at 11. We could have a preview in the morning, 9 to 11."

"Yeah, I like the idea. When?" Joe replied. They both looked at the calendar. "October 20? That's a little over three weeks. Can we pull it together by then?"

"I think so," said Lynn. "I will see if I can line up an auctioneer. We'll use that side room as the staging area and then have it on the porch if it isn't raining. If it rains, I guess we need a backup plan. We also need a banner and some advertising."

"I can take care of that," Joe hurried to get started.

On a Friday just before closing time at 5 pm, Lynn looked up to see Dan Taylor at the door. Uh oh, she thought. He came to the counter with the ring box in his hand.

"Can I return this? he said.

"No, I am sorry, we have a no return policy. It's posted there by the door. The best we can do is take it as a new consignment." Lynn paused. "I am so sorry. May I ask what happened?"

"She said she didn't like it, it was too old, she wants something new. I decided I didn't like her reaction. So that was that." He shook his head sadly.

"I am sorry. Would you like to consign it?"

He thought for a few minutes. "No," he replied. "I think I'll keep it as a reminder."

She nodded. "We are planning to have an auction on October 20, so if you are needing any furnishings, you may want to come over."

"Yes, I'll do that," Dan replied.

Lynn watched him walk out the door as Joe back came in. "So you were right. A mother's instinct at work again," He smiled.

The next morning, shortly after Lynn opened, a young women came into the shop. Lynn figured she was in her mid-twenties. "Hi, I'm Jenny Duncan, Robert Duncan's granddaughter. I understand my grandfather consigned a set of china here a couple weeks ago. Is it still here?"

"No, I'm sorry, it was sold within a few days after he

brought it in," Lynn replied.

"Darn it! I just got back from overseas and my Dad pushed him to sell it without talking to me. I wanted that china! I loved it! Oh, I am so pissed." She fell silent. "I'm sorry, I shouldn't be taking this out on you. But this just makes it final, I can't stay with dad anymore, I need my own place. I am sorry to bother you." She turned to leave.

Lynn stopped her. "We get lovely sets of china in here all the time, mostly because the kids don't want them. Some are exquisite. Please stop back and take a look. And we have our Auction coming up October 20. I'm sure we'll have some sets in that. We also have everything a young person needs to set up a new place. I hope you will come back."

"Maybe I will," Jenny smiled warmly.

Lynn walked over to the door to the backroom. Joe was just getting in. "Not a great way to start a weekend," she said." A granddaughter pissed at her dad for selling grampa's china out from under her. Families are such a mess."

Saturday was busy with lots of Browsers in the shop and the Autumn Leaf Festival going on in town. By

Monday, Lynn looked forward to a little break when she could tidy up the place. She had just gotten started in the side room when she heard the door open. A middle-aged man placed a large box on the table.

"Hi, Lynn," said the man.

"Well, hi to you, too, John Franklin. What brings you into my shop?" replied Lynn. "I haven't seen you since I retired. How is the English department doing these days?"

"All is well at school. I took the morning off, but things have been a little hard for me. My sister Maria died a few weeks ago. She had nobody else but me, so now I am trying to clean out her little house to get it sold. I thought I'd start with clothes, but maybe Joe can come by with his truck and take a look at the furniture one of these days. It's all nice stuff."

"Yes, he can do that. We have an auction coming up October 20th and some nice furniture would be good in it. Let's see what you have." Lynn opened the box and pulled out a pile of cotton and cashmere sweaters. "These are good, and timely for right now with winter coming."

"There are several different sizes. She got smaller as

she got older. There are other clothes below them."

Lynn sorted the clothes into piles and tallied up the consignment, "How is your family?"

John looked down uncomfortably. Lynn stopped and waited. "Maybe you didn't hear, I lost my wife Lizzie two years ago. No, she didn't die. She just left, after 30 years of marriage, she just packed her things and left." He looked bewildered. "I still don't understand it and the divorce was final a year ago."

"I am so sorry to hear that. I always thought she was an interesting woman. Are the kids okay?"

"Yeah, they are off at school now and busy with their lives. It really has just been an adjustment for me."

"I believe that, and losing your sister now," Lynn replied. "It will take some time."

"Well, at least I have things to keep me busy. I'd better get back to school. Let me know when Joe can come over to Maria's house for the furniture." John picked up the consignment paperwork and headed out the door.

Lynn watched him go with some sadness. John had been a new teacher when she was midway through her career and she always liked his enthusiasm for the job. He seemed so adrift now. You just don't know what life is going to throw at you sometimes, she thought.

Lynn and Joe began to get ready for the auction. They moved pieces in and out of the side rooms. They tried to create some space for people to stand inside in case it rained. Joe arranged to pick up Maria's furniture Wednesday.

Early in the week before the auction a woman came in mid-day. "Hi. I don't suppose you remember me. I worked in the front office of the high school about 20 years ago, I was Carol Blake then. Carol Wellington right now," said the woman. She was petite and still cute, with a blonde bob, going slightly gray.

Lynn figured she was in her mid-50s. She did not remember her, but carried on the conversation. "Nice to see you again. What can I help you with?"

"This is hard for me. I have never been in this position before. I am starting over and will pretty much need everything for a very small apartment. But I don't want this to be widely known."

She noticed Lynn's puzzled expression. "Let me

explain. My husband, Marcus Wellington, died last month. You may have read about it, he was quite well-known in town. I was his second wife and we had no children. The children of his first wife have been just hateful to me. I just found out he never did a new will, so I find myself out on the street, literally. I have to find a new place to live by the end of the month." She paused to collect herself. "I may have found an apartment and I just got a clerical job at town hall. But I will need all new furniture and household stuff."

"We can help with that," said Lynn. "We have a consignment of furniture coming in this week on Wednesday for the auction on Saturday. I assume you don't want to be bidding at an auction. We could arrange for you to see it before it goes into the sale. We can substitute other things we have on site as long as we get it done before Friday. The preview is Saturday morning. Can you come in Wednesday afternoon?"

"Yes, after 3. I work until then."

"How about 4?" said Lynn.

After Carol Wellington left, Lynn made her way to the back room to discuss the logistics of the furniture delivery with Joe. "This woman needs some furniture."

"I heard," said Joe.

"So have John come with you after 3 to bring it here. He can help unload."

Joe looked up at her. "I think you're meddling again."

Early Wednesday morning Lynn finished cleaning out the side room that was to be used as the staging area for the auction. Over the weekend they had gone through the shop and tagged items to be sold in the auction. Before starting the job of moving things, she stepped outside to see the red and white banner announcing the auction, waving in the breeze. It was getting a lot of attention. People at the grocery even stopped to talk to her about the auction.

Joe pulled up to the door of the shop in his pick-up truck about 3:15. John followed in an SUV. The two began to carry furniture into the side room. Lynn stood by with a clipboard and noted the items being consigned. Shortly before 4 Carol pulled in behind John's SUV. She made her way into the shop and watched the two men carry in the last of the items. She circled the room with a little note pad. Lynn walked over as the men stopped to rest.

"John, this is Carol Wellington, the one I told you about who has to furnish a new place. Carol, this is John Franklin. He teaches English at the high school. His sister died recently; these are her things."

Carol reached out to shake John's hand. "Carol Blake. I am going back to my old name."

John looked closely at her. "Did you use to work at the school, in the office? You look familiar."

Carol smiled, "Yes, yes, I did but that was over twenty years ago. I can't believe you remember that."

"I never forget a pretty face," John replied with a grin.

Lynn stepped in, smiling to herself. "Carol, what are you interested in?"

"Definitely the little desk and the recliner, a couple lamps, maybe the bed. And I need kitchen stuff. The apartment I am looking at is very small, though," she replied. "But I don't get that place until November 1. Is there some place I can store things until then?"

John responded promptly, "Maybe I could store those things in my garage until you move into your place.

Where will you be living?"

"The apartments near City Hall. That way I can walk to work."

Lynn and Carol wrote up her purchases, while John helped Joe move a few more items into the side room. Then they moved the few things Carol was buying into Joe's SUV.

"Carol, why don't you follow me back to my house where we can unload these," John remarked.

"Sounds good," she replied.

As they walked out onto the sidewalk Lynn heard John say, "Maybe we can get dinner after that."

Lynn chuckled as she turned back into the shop.

"Pretty proud of yourself, aren't you," Joe laughed.

There was no need for a rain contingency plan on Saturday. The day would be a spectacular Fall day. Dan Taylor put the cash into his wallet as he left the ATM. He walked down the block, turned the corner, and saw the Good Things Banner in front of him. He checked his watch, about 20 minutes to go. He walked briskly up the block.

Jenny Duncan entered the shop and stopped to look

around. Lynn was there instantly. "Hi, Jenny. I am so glad you came today. How are things going with you? Did you find a place? And how is your grandfather?"

"Oh, thanks for asking!" replied Jenny. "Things are going well. I found a place over in Silvercreek near Grandpa's place so I can visit him regularly. He is doing much better than I expected. There are several ladies there who try to take care of him and he is loving the attention," she laughed, "especially this one, Anna, who has gotten him back into fishing."

"That sounds very good," said Lynn, smiling to herself. "Let me show you a few sets of china we have in this sale." She and Jenny walked over to the other side of the room.

Dan Tayler appeared in the doorway waving at Lynn. "Dan, nice of you to come. Have you figured out what you need? I am sure we have something for you," Lynn waved back. "Oh, and let me introduce you to Jenny Duncan. Jenny, this is Dan Taylor, a new science teacher at the high school."

Jenny reached out her hand. "Hi. I'm new here, too. I just started working for an environmental consulting firm over in Crosswood, but my family has been around here for a long time."

Lynn left them to talk and welcomed more customers at the door.

Jenny and Dan were looking over the china. "I am looking for a set of china. My family china got sold out from under me," Jenny explained "This one is nice, only 8 place settings, but my grandparents' set was probably too big for me. It was a 12-place set. I don't even know that many people."

"Wow," Dan grinned, "I can't believe we are talking about china sets. I thought I was the only person my age that was into vintage china."

Lynn moved to the center of the room. "Thank you all for coming. We will begin the auction shortly. Please make sure you have signed in and gotten a bidding number, over there by the register. All sales are final. There will be a 10% auction fee on every purchase to pay for the service of Chuck, our auctioneer. Chuck moves very quickly, keep your wits about you and know what you are bidding on. There will be no do-overs! Please make your way to the porch and the front yard once you have signed in."

The auction began and moved at a pace so fast that Lynn had to signal for timeouts to keep up with recording the sales. Dan bid on a desk that he won and a bookcase that he lost.

About an hour into the sale, they got to the china. The auctioneer, Chuck, continued. "So, ladies and gentleman, here we have a nice 8-piece place setting of porcelain with lots of side dishes. Who will start us off on this? Do I have $50, 40, c'mon now, 25? Jenny raised her card. "Who will give me $50?" Immediately a card was raised on the other side of the porch. Jenny and Dan looked over to see who was bidding.

"Do I have 75? Who'll give me 75?" Jenny looked at Dan and frowned, then raised her card.

"I don't think I can go any higher," she whispered. Across the porch came the bid for $100.

"I can help, keep going," replied Dan.

"We are at 100, who will give me 125?"

Jenny looked at Dan. He nodded. She raised her card.

"OK, 150?" Chuck looked over to the other side of the porch. The bidder shook his head no. "Anybody else?

$125 to number 45!" Chuck banged his gavel on the table.

As the auction ended, Dan and Jenny made their way to join the line to check out at the register with Lynn. Jenny pulled $75 out of her wallet and Dan handed her a $50 bill.

"Thanks, I'll pay you back when I get paid next," she said.

"Or I could co-own a set of china," he said with a smile.

"Maybe we ought to have dinner or something before that," she laughed as they carried the two boxes out of the shop.

Later Lynn and Joe took a break from straightening up the shop. "It was a good sale, don't you think?"

"And another successful matchmaking for you with those two young people?" replied Joe.

"I had nothing to do with that one," she protested. "How was I to know they both like old dishes?"

Jeannette M. Bond

Jeannette Bond is a retired tax lawyer who now focuses on the creative side of life, through art and storytelling. She is an artist who spent a lot of days over 13 years standing under a white tent in various grassy locations selling her watercolors, subject to the vagaries of the weather. Her storytelling goes back three decades, to the time when her two children were small. Her technique was to ask for prompts from them for time of year, time of day, characters, place, and weather and then make up a story on the spot. She recorded these stories on cassette tapes so they could play them at night when she was traveling on business trips.

After living her whole life on the East Coast, she and her husband, Cliff Wymbs, now split their time between Arizona and New Jersey. Her watercolor palette now includes lots of shades of red and brown in addition to all the blues and greens. The settings for her short stories have expanded to include mountain deserts as well as seashore towns and lots of places in between.

The Reunion
By Raymond Brunt

You've managed for all these years to avoid attending one. You give yourself the excuse that, at minimum, it might make good writing material someday. So, you sign up to attend your fiftieth high school reunion.

It's a cool Autumn night, and the leaves are blowing up from behind, skidding past you along the sidewalk. After the hour long drive you feel good to be out of the car and walking. At The Holiday Inn you fold into a line with people you don't recognize, and can't imagine this is the correct line because these people are all so old; so, you make an inquiry and it turns out that you are in the right line. At check-in, each classmate is given a name badge to wear with their high school yearbook photo attached. While fumbling around trying to pin the thing on, you see the world is suddenly young and recognizable again in black and white.

At first you feel awkward, lost, and out of sorts as you cross over into a large somewhat pedestrian banquet room. Your stomach drops, your heart starts to race and you consider walking out unnoticed. Mick is howling "Ruby Tuesday" from the DJ's speakers and you're having trouble actually recognizing anyone, when suddenly someone recognizes you. She says her name is, Barbara Blaise, and she asks if you remember her? Her dress is very blue and very floral, and you can't help but think that, by the way she is struggling not to blink, the length of her false eyelashes must be a choice she is now regretting. You might as well be at someone else's reunion because you have no idea who she is. You squint at her photo and say, "yes, of course I do." But of course you don't. She's very sweet, and says that you were in biology together sophomore year, and how she remembers the day when you slid some frogs designated for dissection in between the blinds while the substitute teacher showed the class a movie about amoebas. After the film, when the substitute raised the blinds, the dead frogs appeared to leap out at him and the poor bastard screamed. Replying that it wasn't you that did it she laughs and says to you in a surprisingly accurate Joan Rivers impersonation, "Oh please! Can we talk? The statute of limitations is up on this one." She begins to laugh then you nervously laugh a little too loud at her joke and begin to fear that your over reaction may further expose her loneliness. Before she has the chance to ask you any more questions you say that you need to get a drink and point toward the bar as you drift away smiling.

After finding the line for the bar you run into a guy you played in a band with when you were in your twenties. He's still wearing his hair long, but now it's shockingly white and tied back in a ponytail. Because he is so much shorter than you it's hard not to take notice that the top of his skull is bald, tan, and gleaming. You imagine him at home getting ready for the evening by buffing it with some sort of special product to achieve this level of sheen. He says, "I'm still out there doing it every weekend, man." He hands you his band's business card and tells you they're playing next week at The Stone Pony, which seems ironic because it's the last place you played together nearly forty years ago. He lowers his voice and glances around secretively as he tells you how he plans on slipping in some originals without the owner noticing. Something he used to pull when you played in wedding bands together back in the day. You ask him what's happened to the other ex-band members, but for some reason he only chooses to tell you about the two that have died. He says, "Give me a call sometime, man. Maybe we can jam together?" And you reply, "definitely man," and as he strides away you hold up his card and wave it in the air like it's a winning lottery ticket that you notice has just caught fire.

You're next in line now at the bar and you order a Belvedere-rocks-olives "but easy on the rocks please." The bartender watches you stuff a fiver into her tip jar, so she fills one glass with vodka, a separate glass with ice, and hands you a plastic spear full of olives. You gulp your drink down enough so you can plop in some cubes along with the olives and you find yourself circling little cliques of classmates, attempting to mingle; on a mission to find someone you know.

You finally recognize a guy you were in Little League Baseball with, Andy, and so you sidle over to where he is holding court. He makes eye contact with you, then looks at your pinned on yearbook photo and smiles. He takes a breather from the story he's telling; he shakes your hand and you say, "wow it's been awhile. What are you doing these days?"

You notice that he has morphed into one of those men whose head now looks ridiculously small for their body, and he tells you he is still selling insurance, but in a tone that makes you wonder if perhaps you were the only person in the room who doesn't know this already. He puts his arm around you in much the same way he did when you struck out that time in the all-star game, only now he says he's selling a new policy that covers funeral costs, and he can get you a discount if you hook up with Larry from the local funeral home. Andy hands you a business card from his jacket pocket and then you get a card handed to you from Larry, the owner of Jenkinson's Funeral Home, who just happens to be standing next to Andy. The vodka has taken effect, so you feel comfortable saying in your best Dracula voice, "ahhh, so it appears that you two have formed a mutually beneficial partnership." Your attempt at humor falls flat, and you wonder if that kid who once tried to console you is held up inside of that expanded torso somewhere.

Now, after collecting several business cards you begin to think that perhaps you should have also brought business cards to pass out too, but you don't actually have a business. Just as you begin to fantasize what ironic things you might have had printed on fake business cards, Andy introduces you to his fiancée, Peggy, and then goes back to telling his audience the story about the glory days. Peggy shakes your hand, smiles and says that she thought your joke was actually funny, and then tells you, "These guys are oblivious. I hear the same stories over and over every time we come to something like this."

Sensing that she is bored and would prefer to be anywhere in the world but here, you decide at that moment to reply with, "she couldn't make it," if anyone asks where your wife is. Peggy looks a good twenty years younger than Andy, which leads you to ask her how long they've been engaged? She rolls her eyes and tells you, "We're not engaged." You feel foolish like maybe you misheard him or something. She says, "He always uses the term fiancée after he's had a few drinks. Once he sobers up, we're back to whatever it is we really are."

Together you stare over at Andy who's yakking it up and you remember when he was catching behind the plate in Little League, and how he used to always chat up the hitters to distract them. As he is telling his story you can see he is really on a roll, and you realize things haven't changed at all. You can tell by his pacing and the rising crescendo that he is about to unleash the punchline. That's when Peggy grabs your arm, looks into your eyes and mouths the words as Andy delivers them, "That's what she said!" Everyone laughs except for Peggy. You say, "It's been really nice meeting you, Peggy." She makes a funny face that only you can see, crossing her eyes as she nods her head toward Andy, and you share a laugh as you slink away.

You notice the buffet is being served and your drink is almost empty, so you decide you'd better get something to eat. In the buffet line, there are mostly couples engaged in conversation with other couples. The former king and queen of the prom, and all the high school sweethearts that never moved elsewhere, who only feel comfortable talking amongst themselves. They are as fearful as ever of the outside world and equally leery of people who have re-entered for a visit.

You get the lemon chicken and rigatoni in vodka sauce, and sit down next to a guy, who, as it turns out you actually were in biology class with. You talk about the time you both took lead pencils to the eye pieces of the microscopes used by those two stuck up girls who refused to talk or be lab partners with you. You laugh harder now than you did back then remembering the sight of their raccoon eyes lifting away from their microscopes.

He lives in Texas now and tells you about how much cheaper it is to live there. He married a girl from Ft. Worth who told him before leaving for the reunion," I've never left Texas my whole life, I'll be damned if I'm gonna leave now."

Just as well, he said and laughed. Before he asks, you volunteer that your wife couldn't make it either. He tells you how he works a backhoe, same as he did after high school. He says, "I could have gone clear down to China with all the holes I've dug; foundations, pipelines, landfills, and more graves than I care to remember."

You notice he talks with a windblown Texas accent now and displays no sign of his original Jersey speak. He says, "I'll never be out of work, eventually everything winds up underground." You reply, "Damn straight, brother," surprisingly adopting his Texas accent as your own.

As he pulls the toothpick from his mouth and spins it between his thumb and forefinger, you notice a fleck of chicken flies off onto his navy-blue polo shirt. You try not to, but your eyes keep getting drawn to it and you feel more and more anxious until you finally excuse yourself. And as you head back to the bar for another drink, he raises his glass to you and yells, "Heres to ya padner!"

As you're standing in line at the bar again, you notice an "In Memoriam" video loop running above the bar with a barely audible Jim Croce singing "Time in a Bottle." The yearbook photos fade in and out as their names drift away from the fading photo. You join in with the moans when popular faces appear and with the shared looks of confusion when others appear that no one remembers. "Car accidents and breast cancer," the guy holding a long neck and standing behind you says. "So far each one has died in either a car accident or from breast cancer."

You don't recognize the guy at all and you're not sure if you're shocked because what he claimed may actually be true or by the way he just blurted it out. "Oh wait, that one's from diving into dark water. Alas the string has been broken," he says. Then after he swigs from his beer, he looks at you like he expects you to laugh along with him and all you can do is raise your eyebrows to their peak height, and keep them raised until the bartender hollers, "Next!"

Marilyn! Hey, Marilyn! You shout halfway across the room and wave frantically after you gulp down some more vodka. Marilyn used to share a cigarette with you under the stairway after lunch junior year on the way to history, until you were both caught and got detention for a month. As you catch up with her and look into the woman's eyes you realize it's not Marilyn at all, but perhaps the wife of some other unknown classmate. You continue past her waving pretending the person you're looking for is deeper into the crowd, until you eventually run into your old friend, Jimmy. Speaking for a few minutes about wood shop class and how he labored all year making a chalice on a lathe, he recalls how it took you just as long to make house numbers for your parents ' home. He mentions that your house number was eleven, and you suddenly get that familiar red-faced feeling of embarrassment you felt almost every day of your life in high school.

He asks if you remember Susie Quinn, and you say, "yeah, they called her Susie Q." Jimmy brings you over to her and you're re-introduced. As you and Susie stare at each other and struggle to remember how you first met, she recalls that you were in fourth grade together. You tell her that coincidently just a few years ago, you were across the street from the old elementary school. You describe how it was being torn down and explain how the wrecking ball that cracked open your old classroom seemingly cracked open your memory as well for the whole world to see. You tell her how you imagined your nine-year-old self sitting in the classroom and imagined what it would have looked like sitting at your desk with the side of the building torn off. You then ask yourself, *Did I just say that out loud?* You feel better when Susie reminds you in her mellow two martini voice that you were both in that classroom together on the day that Kennedy was shot. Then you tell her how you vividly remember her sobbing at her locker next to the teacher who was rubbing her shoulders and kissed her forehead.

She says she can't believe how well your memory is still intact. You respond that the distant past may be all that's still intact, and looking into her eyes you see that she's starting to well up a bit. You ask if she's okay, and she says she's fine. She wipes a tear from her cheek with the flesh of her thumb. Susie stares down into your drink and without warning she explains to you why she doesn't like to get out of bed most mornings. She says, "I find that my dreams have become more interesting and fun than my life. I strain and struggle to stay in my dreams as long as I can every morning. Sometimes I feel as if I'm staring a hole into the back of my eyelids to keep them from fading. But they always do." She says how she thinks way too much about dying some days and you say, "Join the club." That makes her laugh. She then points to the guy with the walnut-shell face at the bar and says that he's her second ex-husband, and that's who she's here with. You say, he looks like a nice enough guy. Susie responds that he's a drunken buffoon, but he drives a really nice car. And that makes you laugh.

After surveying the room together for a minute seemingly with nothing left to say, she asks if your wife came. You prepared all evening for this question, but now you can't swallow, you can't speak and she looks up and sees the combination of panic and grief in your face. She grabs your hand and holds it tightly, as if she's trying to steady her balance, but soon realize she's trying to steady you. She finally breaks the silence and asks if you can remember the name of the fourth-grade teacher? You tell her you'll have to think on it for a minute. She interlocks her fingers in between yours now and squeezes your hand even harder. You try and catch her eye but now she's glancing off into the crowd of old classmates. You follow her gaze and watch the same people dancing to Don McLean's "American Pie." Some classmates on the sidelines are starting to yawn, while others are struggling to stand any longer.

As you're about to tell her you don't think you remember the teacher's name, the girl from the pinned on black and white photo comes to life. You feel her smile warm the side of your face. She lets go of your hand and quickly unpins your class photo and name badge from your lapel and places it into her purse. Then she un-pins hers and she slides it into the pocket of your sports jacket. You're caught off guard by this and want to say something clever, but luckily, you're at a loss. She finally tells you, "Her name doesn't matter, they're playing my song." The DJ is now blasting Creedence Clearwater Revival's "Susie-Q," and she's laughing as she drags you along, banging shoulders, knocking people's drinks; gliding past more unrecognizable oval voids. They all seem to be gazing into the distance, or maybe into the past at something other than your spirits slithering through the crowd, not a care in the world, inching your way out onto the dance floor.

"And besides," she tells you as she looks you straight in the eye, "tonight, all the time in the world belongs to us."

Raymond Brunt

Ray has been a life long writer who had poetry and short stories published in college literary magazines in the 70's, but only began to take it more seriously later in life. In his early sixties he went to graduate school and received his MFA in Creative Writing - Fiction from The University of Nevada Reno, at Lake Tahoe. His thesis was a collection of linked short stories titled, "The Dying Dreams of a Steely Dan Fan."

He is currently studying screenwriting and adapting one of the stories from this collection into an episodic TV series. He supports his passions for the arts, education and writing by serving on the boards of The Rattlestick Theater in NYC, Project Write Now, a writers institute based in NJ, as well as the Deans Advisory Council for The School of Humanities and Social Sciences at his alma mater, Monmouth University.

Beholden to the Sea
By JD Clapp

Cruising at 20 knots, Peter and I bullshitted about our banner day of tuna fishing. The Coronado Islands lay seven miles ahead, shimmering in the late afternoon sun, waves crashing on their steep rock banks, blasting white spray into the air. I cracked a second Modelo tallboy for Pete.

The collision sounded like a shotgun blast. I thought *rock*, quickly realizing that was impossible. I felt the boat go air born, heard the prop spinning wildly, purchasing nothing but air while the motor screamed. I watched the over-sized kill bag, 500 pounds of fish and ice in all, break loose from the bow and slam into the portside hull wall of Peter's 22' center console. I remember thinking *oh shit* when she landed, the portside gunwale diving under the surface before we pitchpoled.

***

I vomited sea water. Confused, I treaded water,

gagging and coughing, my throat on fire. When the coughing jag stopped, I swam for the Igloo cooler, the only thing floating nearby. Clinging to the cooler, I caught my breath.

Fifty feet away, the bow bobbed just above the surface. Paralyzed by indecision, I debated swimming for it, but feared the sinking boat would drag me down with it. I used the cooler as a makeshift kickboard to retrieve a floating life jacket and water bottle from the small debris field.

"Peter! Peter!"

There was no response.

"Peter!"

I called for him long after I knew there would be no response.

Beyond being professional acquaintances and our mutual love of fishing, I barely knew the man; it was the first time we had fished together.

Seconds later, the water 30 yards to my portside exploded. Startled, I turned to see a gray whale violently thrash the surface, its tail repeatedly slapping, displaced water raining down on me. I watched the whale suffer in fits and starts. Brief periods of violent thrashing gave way to longer spells, the whale still, weakly blowing air through its blowhole in tortured rasps and wheezes. Eventually, with a final thrash, the whale succumbed, then peacefully floated.

Shortly after the whale died, still clutching the cooler, I watched the prow go under. Behind it, Peter floated face-down, bobbing amid whirlpool swirls produced by the sinking boat's vacuum pull. When the swirls stopped, the water boiled large air bubbles escaping from the submerged hull. Eventually all that remained was Peter's half submerged body shimmering in a rainbow sheen of gasoline and motor oil staining the surface.

Watching his corpse, I went numb. Time passed unnoticed, my mind in a detached, stoned, blankness. The sun set. *There was no green flash*, I thought. My skin gooseflesh, I shivered. My hands and arms cramping, my fingers tinged white from my death grip, holding on to the cooler became tenuous. As the sky darkened, my fear approached panic. I shook violently.

Eventually, my mind came back to me, and I took stock of my situation. I was 22 miles south of U.S. waters.

Making the islands using the cooler was untenable. Donning the life jacket draped over my shoulder would require letting go of the cooler, a move I thought too risky. I couldn't hold the cooler much longer. My adrenaline subsiding, the sun gone, cold radiated from my skin into my bones. I feared hypothermia lurked.

Then my mind shifted to the dead whale. Its death throes had echoed out into the sea like a dinner bell, its blood in the water an invitation to the feast. Sharks would eventually come. *If I don't get out of the water, I'm dead*, I thought.

Being the only viable port in my shitstorm, I headed for the dead whale. I shoved the water bottle into my shorts waist band, ran my arm through the life jacket, and let go of the cooler and swam for the whale. The whale's skin, cold, rubbery, and dotted with patches of barnacles, cut and abraded my hands and legs as I climbed up the whale's head onto its broad back.

In the dimness, I saw the source of the whale's demise: A prop much bigger than ours had cut a huge gash running from the baleen of whale's left jaw, across its massive head, ending just above its right eye. Probably near death when we collided, the whale had been just under the surface.

Wed to the whale now, I watched the cooler float away into the night. *How long does a dead whale float?* I wondered as I pulled on the life jacket. The jacket had a whistle clipped to the zipper, a strobe light attached to a molly loop on the shoulder, and provided modest warmth, trapping the heat escaping from my core. Now almost dark, I was grateful to be out of the water.

I took a sip of water from the half-full bottle. I would ration it.

Fear came and went in perfect relation to my thoughts. I imagined the coast guard at my front door — the horror and pain on wife's face, my young daughter clinging to her thigh, crying but not yet understanding. I pushed thoughts of home away.

I tried to settle. I took deep calming breaths of the cool, fresh, salt air. Eventually, my mind focused exclusively on the present: gripping with my legs and knees, looking for a ship's Navigation lights on the horizon, flexing my ankles to ward off cramps.

The stars emerged, slightly dulled by the harvest

moon's ethereal light. My leviathan raft floated gently on calm seas.

Straddling the whale, I pushed my knees hard into its flesh to maintain balance. My legs soon ached. I shifted my weight, but it offered little respite from the pain. I feared falling off my improbable life raft more than the pain.

Around 11:00 p.m. sharks came and fed on the fluke and pectoral flippers. Their bumps into the carcass barely noticeable, their splashes more so.

Probably small blues and makos, I reasoned thinking about the sharks I had caught in these waters over the years.

Extremely tired, fear and pain precluded my sleep. The night passed in maddening slow motion. Before dawn, two ships passed within a mile: the Dole ship headed for San Diego; and a container ship likely headed for San Pedro. I blew the whistle and turned on the strobe but went unnoticed. The ships, however, offered a seed of hope.

Someone will see me, I thought, although not fully believing it.

As dawn broke, I finished my water. The sun would soon warm me. Boat traffic would pick up. The sea remained calm. Small blue sharks came and went. The whale sat lower in the water. I cautiously awaited rescue.

Sometime before midday, thinking I would need liquid later and my thirst would override the natural aversion of drinking piss, I tried to kneel on the whale to urinate into the empty water bottle. Too weak to kneel, I almost toppled over into the sea. I carefully sat back down. Dark urine stained my shorts and ran down my thigh onto the whale.

By 1:00 p.m., five fishing boats and two sail boats had passed in the distance, the closest maybe two miles off. Again, despite strobe and whistle I went unnoticed. Certain my wife had already called the Coast Guard, but would she know where to point them? *Nobody will search for me this far into Mexican waters*, I thought.

The afternoon sun warmed and dried me. My legs ached terribly. The acrid scent of decay began to waft up from my once living perch. The day marched on.

Around 4:00 p.m. I became angry. I cursed and pounded the whale with my right first. My knuckles bled;

a piece of barnacle imbedded in my ring finger. My initial feeling of foolishness gave way to cathartic relief. Then imaging someone viewing the scene from above, the absurdity of a crazed man pummeling the dead whale he sat on, I laughed aloud. I laughed until I cried. Fearing tears of self-pity would be a tacit acquiesce to death, I cried for Peter.

"Don't come undone now," I said aloud.

Another sunset came. Again, I noticed there was no green flash. Painfully thirsty, sunburned, my lips cracked and bled. The barnacle cuts on my legs turned rash-red, maybe infected, burning from the saltwater. My right hand swelled from the punches. My gut churned from hunger. My bone-tired leg muscles went numb. My body, shorts, and t-shirt were filthy, stained with blood from fishing, urine, and caked in salt residue.

The sharks returned just after dark. Their bumps more notable than before, the whale felt less stable, even lower in the water. I feared once the sharks devoured the fluke or pectoral flippers, the whale's natural spontoons, the corpse would roll and dump me into the sea. Unsure if air trapped in its lungs or blubber kept the dead whale afloat, I feared it sinking.

At full dark, a thin marine layer turned the glow of a full harvest moon a muted blood-orange shade. The low clouds mercifully held the remains of the day's warmth. Two ships passed around 8:00 p.m., too far off for the whistle or strobe.

After 9:30 p.m., the southerly swell built, mixing with the prevailing westerly swell. The whale slowly gyrated in the confused seas. Exhausted and in pain, I needed to switch positions. I needed rest.

Using the life jacket as a makeshift pillow, I laid flat on the whale, my stomach flush to its back, my arms and legs splayed akimbo to its moist sides. Sleep came suddenly.

I dreamt of being on a small boat, floating among glacial ice fields. The sea was calm. The sun's rays offset the cold air. It felt good. Brown jagged stone cliffs ended in brilliant evergreen pine forests rimming the small ice dotted bay. A bald eagle surfed thermals high above, coming closer, then closer still in a dipping, tightening corkscrew. From below, I felt vibrations then heard the ghostly call of an orca. The unseen orca did not elicit wariness, but oddly a feeling of connectedness. I floated peacefully in my dream, waiting for rescue without fear or want.

I woke at 4:30 a.m. to the thrumming thunder of helicopter rotors. *Thank God*, I thought. My hopes quickly died as the chopper sped past headlong into the night, clearly not searching for a lost man on a dead whale.

At gray light, sharks fed again. Now the carcass shook violently with each bump and tearing bite. Looking down, I watched a large mako take the last of the starboard pectoral flipper, then fade into the deep blue. Thirty feet below at the fringes of visibility, smaller sharks emerged, first appearing as small, distorted flashes, progressively morphing into sharks as they ascended. They fed heavily. The whale sat lower still; my feet barely cleared the water.

Around sunup, my legs and arms spasmed. Dehydration-fueled pains shot through my extremities. Painfully thirsty, my split lips stung, small drops of blood the only moisture in the desert of my mouth. My dry eyes burned. I struggled to hold on. *When the whale rolls, it will be over*, I thought.

At full light, the wind freshened to 15 knots with gusts of 25. The southern swell grew to five feet, bigger rollers mixed in. Wind gusts carved swell crests into spitting white caps. The whale rolled like a broken metronome, small, chopped swings to the port then longer, deeper dips to the starboard. I jammed my first into the open blowhole and like a rodeo rider strapped to a saddle pommel, I prayed I would remain on the beast.

Soon birds arrived to scavenge. Little white terns came first. They dove to the surface their beaks snatching shards of flesh torn lose by the feeding sharks. Gulls came soon after.

Below the surface, sardines drawn in by the shark-produced chum arrived and mixed in with the sharks. Before long, skipjack and mackerel joined the feeding frenzy. As I watched the symbiotic interplay of scavenger, hunter, and prey, I wondered, *how many times had I raced my skiff to such a scene, rod in hand, ready to cast a lure into the fray?*

My life raft diminished, jagged bite by bite. The whale would roll soon, ending it. I felt faint and dizzy. I dry heaved, the retching sending jarring shock waves of pain through me. My panic returned briefly, followed by acceptance. *I am going to die soon,* I thought.

Not wanting to be awake for it, I closed my eyes. I hunched forward, exhaustion took over, and I faded out. In my stupor, I disassociated again, only marginally aware of my body or situation. My sensations of touch and sound muted. My mind pulled me back to the ice dotted bay of my dream. *This is peaceful place to die,* I thought.

In my half dream state, I heard an outboard's throaty whine and distant voices.

Why are they here? I thought.

Then noises grew loader and more urgent before my mind acknowledged them. Dazed, still unsure I was awake, I looked up.

A young man standing on the bow of azure blue panga yelled in Spanish:

"Mira! Mira!"

"Mira allá! Mira allá!!"

The panga drew within three yards. The young Mexican fisherman tossed a bowline my way. Confused, I didn't even reach for it. *Is he real?* I wondered.

I watched with a detached interest as his partner expertly worked the tiller and whipped the boat around portside, coming flush to the whale in the building seas. Displaced by the panga, the puddled baitfish crashed the surface with hundreds of little splashes sounding like buckets of nickels hitting a wood floor. Birds screamed above.

A strong hand reached over, grabbed my arm, and yanked me into the panga. I collapsed on the deck, landing in a pool of bilge water, fish blood, and spilled gasoline. I looked up blankly at the men talking to me excitedly in Spanish.

Seagulls shrieked above them. Their two-stroke outboard purred loudly, sending wafts of exhaust into the air. The VHF radio crackled with a mix of staticky squelch, men yelling emphatically in Spanish; fishermen from San Diego asking for fish reports. *This is real*, I thought, the haze in my mind lifting.

The fisherman pushed the panga off from the whale. The captain pointed the bow east, revved the engine, then headed toward Rosarito. Underway, the fisherman supported my head and held a bottle of water to my damaged lips.

Beholden to these fishmen, the dead whale, the lifecycle of the sea itself, I croaked, "Gracias."

JD Clapp

JD Clapp is a writer and social scientist based in San Diego, CA. His creative writing draws on decades of experience as a keen observer of human behavior through his work as a field alcohologist (someone who studies drinking behavior in natural environments), and an avid outdoorsman and angler. Often set in the contexts he knows best—bars, academia, rural America, and far-flung hunting and fishing locations—his stories examine themes of love, family, loss, hope, and perseverance. He currently writes short-form fiction and creative nonfiction.

JD's creative work has appeared in 101Words, Micro Fiction Mondays Magazine, Free Flash Fiction, Wrong Turn Literary, Scribes MICRO, Café Lit, and Sporting Classics Magazine among several others. His story, One Last Drop, was a finalist in the 2023 Hemingway Shorts Literary Journal, Short Story Competition. He can be reached at www.jdclappwrotes.com.

Drums of War and of Memory Eighty years on from World War 11
By Sarah Elizabeth Das Gupta

We played with anything lying around in those days, months after the war. There were houses to re-build, food production to be stream-lined, families to be re-united or to adjust to their losses as best they could. There were men and women returning to bombed-out city streets, to old market towns, to seaside resorts, to remote villages. A new society waited to rise phoenix-like from the ashes of the old. A National Health Service, a new Education Act, strange little houses called pre-fabs, great churches, like Coventry Cathedral, new tower blocks, new garden cities. In our road, left to our own devices, we children happily made use of the detritus the war had left behind. Instruments of war became instruments of play and entertainment.

Anybody wandering in the neighbouring woods couldn't be blamed for supposing the war was still going on in that pretty corner of Surrey. Bloodcurdling screams and sinister, gas-masked figures suggested hostilities had certainly not ceased. I can remember our leader, Martin, a noisy ten-year-old, had claimed the enemy was passing coded messages through the whispering of the dark, mysterious pines as the wind moaned through their branches. I became so nervous of the woods that I would walk miles to skirt round the edges. A new tenant on a local farm, who rode around the lanes and footpaths on his horse flecked with foam and two muzzled Alsatians padding at his side, inevitably became 'the enemy'. I later felt guilty to learn he was in fact a Jewish refugee from Germany.

Passersby, seeing us with gas masks on the back of our heads drinking Tizer and eating cheese sandwiches, must have found us a bizarre sight. Little did we remember or know about these masks which had been handed out in boxes to all civilians in Britain by 1939. Even babies had masks in which they were placed with just their legs left dangling. There were masks for all contingencies: helmet-like contraptions for invalids and even gas proof prams! Only later did we understand the horrifying use of carbon monoxide, hydrogen cyanide and Zyklon B in the gas chambers of camps like Auschwitz and Bergen-Belsen.

The old ration books which were lying around the house were also recruited into our post-war games. We set up an improvised shop at the bottom of our garden. Empty tar barrels formed the basic foundations while old planks were laid across to serve as shop counters. Empty bottles, which had once contained rations of orange juice or the much detested, cod liver oil, were filled with bizarre, coloured water. Brilliant concoctions of purple, green and blue water were marked off and recorded in the old ration books. There was the occasional treat of cardboard-like biscuits, still a rarity, even after the war.

Most of our street 'gang' had been born during or just after the war ended. Rationing which began with petrol in 1939 and food in 1940 had always been part of our wartime childhood. Posters calling on civilians to 'Grow Your Own Food' and 'Dig for Victory' were common. Every individual, including children, had a ration book with coupons for such food as sugar, fats, meat, bacon, and cheese. Free milk and eggs for children and pregnant women were a priority. I remember in my village primary school in winter, bottles of frozen milk being lined up round an old Victorian range to thaw. Rationing didn't stop in 1945. In fact, bread was rationed for the first time in 1946. Meat was the last food to be de-rationed. in the early fifties. When my mother married in 1939, she made her own dress out of parachute silk. At least six brides were married in that same dress, with a few minor adjustments. Despite rationing and such culinary delights as 'Patriotic Pudding' and 'Victory Flan', an improved diet for most people resulted in a decline in infant mortality. The truth is the nation overall was probably fitter then, than either before, or since, the war.

Air-raid shelters provided essential protection to the civilian population, particularly during the Blitz on London. The most common were the Anderson Shelters, named after Sir John Anderson, responsible for air-raid defences just before the outbreak of war. These were built in people's gardens. Half-buried underground, the roofs were covered with a thick layer of earth. Many remained into the fifties, some even surviving till today. Our Surrey village is close to Biggin Hill, the main airfield for the Royal Air Force during the Battle of Britain. There was an air-raid shelter very close to our house. This proved to be a wonderful post war headquarters for the 'gang'. The steps led steeply down into a large underground room, a perfect place to simply 'hang out'. We managed slowly and secretly to furnish this new meeting place. Old chairs, discarded by my mother, found their way underground. One of the boys scavenged an ancient table from the village junkyard. Martin's mother, chatting over the garden hedge, commented that the kids seemed to be breaking a lot of crockery and she was always buying mugs and plates. She'd have been surprised at our underground hoard of china. We could probably have hosted a subterranean dinner party with our motley collection of plates and mugs. The walls were covered with graffiti in various colours. At six years old I found the remains of old love messages tedious. Some of the cartoons and writing were totally mysterious and enigmatic, although the older boys seemed to find them more interesting. When I look back at those sepia memories, I sometimes wonder what happened to all those underground artists. How many of them ever returned?

As we enjoyed our underground Head Quarters, we knew nothing of the Bethnal Green disaster in London's East End which led to more deaths, either before or since, than any other tragedy on the metro/tube and no train was involved! Dinners were half-eaten, baths left running on the evening of March 3, 1943 in that working class area of the East End. Hundreds responded to a wailing siren, signaling an air raid. The underground stations had hitherto proved effective in protecting thousands of civilians during attacks on the capital. In Bethnal Green the station had become a social hub. It had canteen facilities and several marriage receptions had been held there. That fateful evening, just as crowds surged down the steep steps towards safety, loud explosions suggested bombs were already falling. Rumours that Hitler had developed a new, more deadly weapon, panicked the crowd even more. A mother with a baby in her arms tripped, a man pushing from behind fell too. In seconds crowds had fallen down the concrete steps leading into the station. One hundred and seventy people died that evening, including sixty- two children. The tragedy seemed even more terrible when it emerged that there had been no air raid. The explosions had come from anti-aircraft guns being tested in a nearby park. The truth surrounding the disaster was kept secret for thirty years.

Oblivious of that horror, we sat in our Anderson Shelter, planning campaigns, drinking lemonade and drawing 'military' maps of the surrounding woods and fields. We had strategies to interpret the secret whispering of the trees and stalk unsuspecting Mr Kinzburg with his sinister, muzzled Alsatians.

The fact that our village was so close to Biggin Hill, had certain implications during the war years. German aircraft flew over southern England during the Blitz on London. On the return flight, to conserve fuel, they dropped any ammunition remaining, on targets between London and the Channel. One of our fields had, and still has, a large crater caused by such somewhat haphazard 'targeting'.

While out walking, over sixty years later, I fell into conversation with an old man scything nettles in his garden. He remembered Messerschmitts flying low over the fields. He had been ploughing with a fine team of chestnut Suffolk Punches (heavy, draught horses). He quickly led them into a nearby wood and watched the bombers streaming overhead. Certainly, a moment in history when the past and present met.

Barrage Balloons were one method of air defence deployed in the war. These were over nineteen metres long and eight metres in diameter, filled with hydrogen to get them airborne. These Frankenstein-like monsters were tethered by metal cables to concrete blocks set securely into the ground. Pilots flying bombers at over three hundred miles an hour, would not have seen this hazard before the metal cables brought the aircraft down, ripped off a wing, or fatally damaged the fuselage. If pilots tried to shoot the balloons down, they risked being caught in the explosion of hydrogen used to launch them.

As a result, German pilots were forced to fly higher, which reduced their accuracy when attacking key targets. Every school pupil has heard of the Battle of Britain pilots, the heroic 'few', famously praised by Churchill. The members of Balloon Command are perhaps the unsung heroes and heroines of the war air defence. In

1941 for the first time, women became full members of the armed forces. Many barrage balloon sites were run by women. Despite initial doubts in some quarters, female crews became expert at launching these monsters. In a nearby field one of these balloons remained for some time after the war ended. It looked rather strange, fenced off but surrounded by horses peacefully grazing. Our gang invented wonderful legends and myths surrounding this tethered, puffed-up giant. Sometimes it was one of the mysterious, secret weapons the Nazis had been rumoured to possess. More often it housed aliens from Mars or beyond. In the early morning mist, or the fading evening light, it seemed to my six -year-old imagination more than possible that little green men might very well emerge. On a windy day, it appeared frustrated, like a strange creature pulling angrily at the wires restraining it. Perhaps, it dreamed of those past, perilous nights when the bombers had streamed overhead towards London?

In some ways I felt closer to the war through my maternal grandparents. They lived in a large house and had young pilots billeted on them throughout the war.

My grandmother told me that the majority were killed within three weeks. Very few survived to 1945. I felt glad that my grandmother was a fabulous cook, that my grandfather challenged them to tennis matches, which they invariably won, and that 'Kilbernie' was a beautiful house surrounded by the open countryside of the North Downs.

Some evenings during the Blitz, my grandparents, with my mother and me, then a toddler, would stand in the woods at the back of the house, watching dog fights between individual aircraft. One brilliant, moonlit night, we saw a German plane shot down and a pilot with the crew bailing out. My mother told me years later that they were very young and frightened. They seemed almost pleased to surrender to the local police. She said she had imagined Dad, somewhere in the Mediterranean on the dangerous Malta Convoys. Not for the first time, she had thought how tragic and futile war is.

Even eighty years on, these memories are still as clear as if they had happened yesterday. I have often wondered if our war games influenced our later lives and personalities. I look at many youngsters today sitting indoors on a bright, sunny day, playing war games on a computer. I feel our outdoor, inventive play in all the vagaries of the British weather, probably did us less harm than good. It has certainly not drawn me towards violence.

My final image of the war was seeing a German prisoner helping with haymaking on a local farm. He and the farmer's teenage son were lifting bales of hay and loading them onto a trailer. Suddenly the tractor driver moved off and the bale of hay was left hanging from the back at a dangerously rakish angle. The two were convulsed with laughter.

Sarah Elizabeth Das Gupta

Sarah Das Gupta was born in 1942 so is a war baby, rather than a baby boomer. She remembers gas masks, ration books, air shelters becoming part of her post-war childhood. The first film she saw was Lawrence Olivier's iconic production of Henry V, dedicated to the Battle of Britain pilots, which was shown on the walls of a makeshift classroom. She graduated from London University in 1962 with a degree in History and trained as a teacher. The next years she spent in Kolkata (Calcutta), married to a Bengali journalist. These were exciting times, teaching and adjusting to a new life and culture. Now in her eighties, with the support of her two daughters and five wonderful grandchildren, she has started writing after a spell in hospital following an accident. Her work has been published in over fifty magazines and anthologies in ten countries.

The Password
By Edward E. Douglas

Franz reached the tiny hut in the middle of the forest after a half-hour hike on a seldom-used trail. His grandfather had sent him on a mission. "Follow that trail until you reach a pond. In a clearing beside it, you'll see a shabby little hut. Say to the man living there, *'Kleine lerchen hinken.'* That's the password. It means "Little larks limp." The man will answer, *'Dann sollten sie fliegen.'* That's the countersign. It means—"

"I speak German too, Opa," said Franz. "It means *'Then they should fly.'"* Grandpa's native language was German, but in college he achieved fluency in English, although he only swore in German. Franz was naturally bilingual, having spent his first five years in America and the next five in Germany.

"Mr. Schwartz lives alone in that hut." Grandpa said, "He's in the Resistance. He's on our side and will welcome you and give you a package to bring back to me. Can you do that?"

Franz nodded and did as his grandfather instructed, but as he approached the hut, it seemed nobody was around. He called out, "Ist da jemand?" He stood silently listening; leaves rustled in the breeze and frogs croaked in the pond. He smelled decaying vegetation. It was a warm spring day, but an icy chill ran down his back.

He walked warily to the door, found it unlatched and slightly ajar. He tried both languages. "Ist da jemand? . . . Is anybody there?" No answer. The door opened easily with a gentle push. He peered inside. The only light came through one small window. On a table sat a portable kerosene cookstove. The floor was hard-packed dirt strewn with straw. Against the opposite wall was a military-style cot, and on it lay a man who appeared to be asleep. "Kleine lerchen hinken," Franz said, softly at first, then again louder, expecting the man to awaken and respond, but the room remained silent. It was then Franz noticed blood seeping from a wound on the man's chest. Franz trembled and wished his grandfather were there to tell him what to do.

The boy's mouth felt like he'd tried to swallow

cotton. His stomach was queasy. He cautiously approached and felt the man's neck for a pulse. There was none. He assumed this was Mr. Schwartz, the man who would have answered his password with *'Dann sollten sie fliegen,'* and given him the package, except someone murdered him and might have also stolen the package. He searched the hut, hoping the dead man had concealed it before they killed him. The phrase "needle in a haystack" crossed his mind. A small pile of straw in the corner resembled hay. He scattered the pile with his foot and found a small manilla envelope concealed underneath. He hoped it was the package Grandpa sent him for.

Franz scooped it up, shoved it under his shirt, exited the hut, and jogged down the trail. Halfway to the trailhead, he heard a shout, then gunfire. A bullet knocked bark off a nearby tree. Stark fear accelerated his pace into a sprint, which he kept up until he felt a sharp pain in his side. He panicked, thinking he'd been shot. He fell to his knees and crawled behind a tree. He waited, listening for gunfire, but the pain in his side slowly subsided, and he realized it was just a muscle spasm. He resumed running toward where Grandpa waited at the trailhead in his wheelchair.

When Grandpa saw Franz run out of the woods, he shouted his name. Franz slowed to a walk, wheezing from exertion. Sweat glistened on his face. He bent with hands on knees until he could summon enough breath to speak.

"Is this the right package?" Franz handed it to Grandpa, who hid it, as Franz had, under his shirt.

"Let's hope to God it is. Any problems getting it?"

"The man in the hut was dead. He had hidden it, but I found it. As I ran back here, someone shot at me."

Grandpa's normally stoic face reddened, and he spoke harshly. "Gott im Himmel! You say Herr Schwartz is dead? And who would shoot at a 10-year-old boy? Idioten! Arschlöcher! Are you okay?"

"I'm okay, Opa."

"Then let's get going. Give me a push." Franz grabbed the handles of the wheelchair and pushed it onto the hard-packed gravel road leading toward town. Grandpa could walk, but arthritis in his hips restricted him to short distances. He was grateful for his grandson's assistance.

The two soldiers manning the guard-post recognized the old man and boy. They had inspected identification papers earlier when the boy pushing the old man in a wheelchair left the village. Grandpa had told a convincing lie. Displaying his medical bag, he said, "I need to check on an ailing widow lady in a farmhouse not far away." They had given his bag a thorough inspection and sent them on their way with a stiff-armed "Heil Hitler" salute. This time they judged the pair insignificant and waved them on. Franz pushed the wheelchair past the soldiers. Their destination was two blocks further, a big brick building on a quarter-block lot with out-buildings and a garden—Dr. Franz Dietrich's residence and clinic. To young Franz it was just "Opa's house."

Although retired and handicapped, Dr. Dietrich provided what medical care he could for those who remained after able-bodied men and women joined the army or took manufacturing jobs to support the war. No one would guess he worked for the Resistance. He was the trusted and beloved physician they referred to as

"Herr Doctor."

The boy was born in America. His mother, a foreign exchange student at New York University, met and married Jim Roberts, an American. When Franz was four, his mother developed a rare form of cancer and died a year later. His father, training as a pilot in the U.S. Army Air Corps, sent Franz to live with his maternal grandfather in Germany several years before the war began. With Hitler's war now endangering civilians, Grandpa desperately wanted to send Franz to a safer place. The package would help make that possible.

Grandpa fixed a supper of salt-pork, spätzle, and fresh spargel—white asparagus grown in his garden. For a special treat, they enjoyed apfelstrudel made with home-canned apples. They went to bed early because the next day would be both trying and tiring.

A rooster's crow awakened Franz at dawn. After serving Franz a simple but filling breakfast, Grandpa laid the now open manilla envelope on the table. "Change of plans, Franz. I opened the package, and yes, it's the right one. Our spies within the German command gained copies of these documents and smuggled them to me.

They reveal the schedule and route a German army division will advance toward Allied troops. I had intended to trade these strategic plans to the Americans or British for your safe passage to England or America, but the information is urgent. It can't wait for personal delivery to our Allied contacts. I must radio them immediately."

Grandpa left Franz doing customary morning chores while he laboriously climbed the stairs to the second floor. He struggled up a rickety ladder into the attic where he activated an illegal radio-transmission station.

"Little larks limp. Little larks limp," he said into the microphone.

Out of the static came a garbled response. "Then they should fly. Go ahead, little lark."

"The cattle resting in the barns of Sydney for the second night are fat enough for market." Sydney was the current code name for Grandpa's village. Only high command and trusted agents knew the codes, which frequently changed. Grandpa's message was deliberately obscure to confuse German intelligence officers who listened to all radio transmissions. Allied command would understand. Grandpa's coded message requested an air attack on his own village two nights from now. Soldiers, tanks, and armament moving toward the front would camp overnight in their town. They'd be sitting ducks if the Allies knew exactly where they were.

Dr. Dietrich had lain awake for hours struggling with the decision. His home could be destroyed, but which was more important—his house or a strategic victory for the Allies? No village on the route-plan of the Nazis was a better choice. It had no air-raid sirens or powerful searchlights. No anti-aircraft guns would be in place except a few on trucks accompanying the convoy. This was the least likely place where German strategists might expect an attack.

Making his way back to the ground floor, Grandpa said, "Franz, we haven't time to waste. I need you to warn the people. Go to my garden and pull lots of radishes. Tie them in bunches, about a handful in each. Load them in your wagon and go house to house, but only where villagers live—not where soldiers are quartered. Knock on doors and give each resident a bunch of radishes. Say, in German, of course, '*Doctor*

Dietrich sends a gift and warns that Allied planes will attack two nights from now.' Everyone knows you're my grandson, and they'll know to evacuate the village."

"Why am I doing this, Opa? What's happening?"

"Tanks, portable artillery, ammunition haulers, and marching men with rifles and grenades will take over the village. They'll park their heavy machines in people's yards to leave the streets open. Officers will commandeer a building—courthouse, school, or church—to use as their headquarters. Soldiers will sleep in every available bed. They'll confiscate all the food, rob every wine cellar, search every house, garden, and outbuilding, and take anything they want."

"But won't the soldiers be suspicious if the villagers have left?"

"No. They're used to finding empty villages. They're pleased that everyone's afraid of them and gets out of their way."

Franz understood why Opa entrusted him with this mission. His grandfather couldn't walk well enough to go house to house, and it would appear suspicious if he did. A ten-year-old boy, giving away radishes to friends and neighbors, would not. Franz did as he was told. He finished the task by noon.

His workday was not over. He spent the afternoon carrying boxes of medical records to the cellar, along with anything else Opa wanted stored in a safer place. When night came, Franz was so tired he fell asleep on the living room couch while Opa played gramophone records of Beethoven symphonies. He didn't wake until dawn the next day.

After breakfast, Grandpa led the boy to a dilapidated shed behind the house to reveal under a dusty, weathered tarp an ancient motorcycle. He directed Franz to wheel it out, and together they washed it, oiled it, aired its tires, and filled its tank from a can of gasoline squirreled away before the war began.

The motorcycle had a sidecar. Since Grandpa couldn't sit astride the machine, he would ride in the sidecar. Franz would have to drive. Opa spent the next two hours giving Franz driving lessons. He taught Franz as much as he could without running the motor, but he let Franz start the noisy engine and drive it around the house several times. Franz was quick to learn and big and strong for his age, often mistaken for a twelve or fourteen-year-old. "Look at me, Opa! It's like riding a bicycle, only bigger. I can drive the motorcycle just fine."

At dusk, Grandpa loaded his medical bag and travel necessities. Franz helped him into the sidecar, started the motorcycle, and slowly maneuvered out onto the street. He did as Opa told him. He drove around the town square toward the edge of town opposite his grandfather's home. They heard the roar of tanks, trucks, and motorcycles approaching the village from the south. Those machines led the way for hundreds of marching soldiers.

As they reached the north edge of town, they expected to be stopped, and they were.

"Halt!" A soldier raised his bayonet-affixed rifle.

Grandpa said to him in German, "A young woman in the next town sent word she has gone into labor. I must go deliver her baby." He lifted his medical bag so the sentry could see it.

"Of course," said the soldier, who clicked his heels, gave the Nazi salute with an exuberant "Heil Hitler," and motioned them to proceed. Grandpa rolled his eyes at

Franz, and both responded in kind without enthusiasm. Failure to return the salute would have aroused suspicion.

They didn't go to the next town. Grandpa and Franz rode to a hill overlooking the town from which they could see townsfolk carrying away what belongings they could. They weren't walking on roads, but along hedges and through fields and vineyards surrounding the town. That satisfied Opa. His people were moving to safety.

Franz drove the motorcycle, as Opa directed, to a grove of trees on the crest of a hill five miles away. They waited, watched, and listened.

At midnight a squadron of bombers and fighter planes approached, buzzing like a swarm of bees. With mixed emotions, Franz and Opa watched the deadly fireworks show above the distant village. Tracer bullets painted glowing lines across the darkness. Exploding bombs flashed, followed seconds later by deep booming sounds muted by distance. The whine of aircraft engines seemed louder than that of the guns and bombs because the planes flew almost over their heads, and assaulted their ears unmuffled by intervening hills and trees. Their shrieks and moans rose and fell in dissonant harmony as they dived, delivered destruction, then climbed to make their escape. Anti-aircraft guns thudded like hammers on hollow barrels. The sickening staccato of fighter plane machine guns buzzed like rattlesnakes. The hum and thrum of engines finally faded as the Allied aircraft sped away. Light from burning buildings reflected off the bottoms of the clouds as the night grew silent again.

Tears came to Grandpa's eyes. He would never return to the village he faithfully served or the home he grew up in, a fine house inherited from his father, where he had raised his own children. He would never again visit the Catholic church he attended all his life and where he wed his wife, who now lay buried in its cemetery.

They spent the rest of the night sleeping on the ground, wrapped in blankets which Grandpa had stuffed into a compartment of the sidecar. At dawn, they drove to the next town and ate breakfast at a tiny café, still in business despite the war. A few more towns away, they felt safe enough to ask how far to the front lines of Allied troops. They bought contraband gas and refilled the motorcycle.

They reached the advancing Allies that evening. Soldiers stopped them at gunpoint, but when Franz called out, "I am an American," they lowered their weapons. Franz dismounted and helped his grandfather out of the sidecar. A soldier summoned an officer, to whom Grandpa explained his status in the Resistance, and that Franz was his American grandson. They sought asylum and transportation to England or America.

"Yeah? You say you work for the Resistance?" said the skeptical officer. His job involved communications, so he knew about the Resistance. He knew their operatives' intelligence had launched last night's raid that crippled the advance of German tanks and troops. He asked for something few knew existed. "So, what's the password, Mister?"

Franz spoke up. "Little larks limp."

Smiling, the officer said, "Then they should fly. Welcome, little lark." He laid a protective hand on Franz's shoulder and gestured to Grandpa. "C'mon to the mess tent, and we'll get you some supper."

***

Epilogue:

The Allies transported Franz and his grandfather to England. There Franz was reunited with his father, Lt. Col. James T. Roberts of the U.S. Army Air Corps stationed there. After the war, the three returned to the United States where old Grandpa Dietrich lived with the Roberts family until his death in 1953.

Having Americanized his first name years ago, Dr. Frank Dietrich Roberts now lives in a suburb of St. Louis, retired after a long career as a physician like his maternal grandfather he'd been named after. He told this story in first-person to his children and later to his grandchildren—how he took part in the Second World War when he was only 10 years old. He always concluded his story with, "And you know what else? My father piloted one of the planes in the squadron that bombed Grandpa Dietrich's village and the Nazis who occupied it."

His grandkids claimed not to believe him, but he knew they really did.

Edward E. Douglas

Ed Douglas retired in 2006 after a variety of professions including Christian ministry, public education, business management, and photography. He has a B.A. in Art, an M.A. in Education, and a year of theological school. He spent 5 years as a Methodist pastor, 27 years teaching English and Art on high school level, and over 25 years in professional photography. In retirement he began writing poetry and short stories for personal enjoyment, taking non-credit courses through OLLI (*Osher Lifelong Learning Institute*) and the *Institute of Children's Literature*. Moving from the Peoria IL area to San Antonio's *Hill Country Retreat* in 2020, he joined the San Antonio Writers Guild and founded the HCR Creative Writing Group which meets bi-weekly in the HCR retirement community. Besides writing, Ed enjoys photography, fishing, and riding his Terra-trike 10 miles a day. He is married and has 3 sons, 5 grandchildren, and 2 great granddaughters.

The Men in the Dunes
By Ellen Herbert

Barbara's gold cross, nestled in the hollow at the base of her throat, glinted in the Saturday sun as I sat between her and her brother, Paul, in the backseat of their family's station wagon. We were on our way to the beach that August day in '67. While the war in Vietnam raged, the hippies' summer of love wound down, and race riots occurred all over America, I was seventeen and mostly unconcerned about the world's problems. My worry was Barbara, my new best friend. With school starting soon, I feared our friendship would not survive returning to separate high school planets—hers, vocational ed and mine, college prep.

Paul, who was reading a book on asteroids, didn't look up when we came to Camp LeJeune's main gate and waited to be waved through by an MP. Barbara's little brothers, Egg and Larry, sat in the back wedged between bags of food and boxes of bed linens.

I needed to beg permission to come along. Fortunately, Mother was working on her doctorate at Carnegie Mellon way up in Pittsburgh, and my dad, a beer-guzzling, poker-playing darling, sorely needed a break from being Mr. Mom. He allowed my sister to go with friends to the mountains.

"It's only fair you let me go," I said, looking deeply into his sky blue eyes. I was building a case for him to present to Mother when she found out later. She didn't approve of Barbara.

"Don't think this is some luxury vacation," Barbara told me when I called her with the news I was coming. "The only reason we are going is because sergeants get to stay in these cottages for free." Her dad's frugality was a constant complaint. Worse, though, was the way he made Barbara feel inferior because she was not book-smart like her brothers. "The nicest thing the cheapo ever says to me is 'At least I won't have to pay for college for you.'"

Unlike Barbara, her brothers were in gifted and talented programs, and Paul, who won a high school science fair while only in junior high, was considered brilliant.

Outside the car windows, the Marine base gave way to soupy marshes edged by bare trees, moss boas dangling from their limbs. As we crossed the Inland Waterway, the bridge rattled beneath us, its seams humming an overture that meant the Atlantic was close. The water gleamed in the morning light as fog rose from it like breath.

Excited, Larry and Egg began to rattle the bags around them.

"Stay still, monkeys, or you'll crush the potato chips," Mrs. Novak called from the shotgun seat.

Her Carolina accent reminded me that she was a local girl who had married the Sergeant, a Pole from Michigan. Mother called such marriages "mixed," something she should know about. She and my dad were as different as saint and sinner could be. I straddled their two worlds, lately preferring Dad's because he was more fun.

Studying the backs of their heads—the Sergeant's chiseled perfection, Mrs. N.'s wild curly hair, so unkempt she might have combed it with an eggbeater—I wondered what force had brought them together. The answer had to be sex: something I knew little about but pondered often.

I sensed my mother was referring to sex when she took me aside after she first met Barbara and told me that Barbara was *an experienced girl* (probably because Barbara bleached her hair and had already started dating.) "So?" I said to Mother. Barbara's experience was what I liked about her. She represented the world to me, more real than anything I could learn from my *World Book Encyclopedia.* I wanted some of Barbara's cool, to know what her knowing eyes knew.

The dunes appeared like giant pillows, their sand encroaching on the strip of road. "It reminds me of the moon's surface," Paul said, glancing up from his book. He was a male version of gorgeous Barbara, blonde with grape green eyes.

"But no one really knows what the moon is like," said Sergeant Novak, secretly called *the commandant* by his family. Paul was the only member of his family that engaged his attention.

"We know the moon is covered in fine dust-like sand created when meteorites strike and explode," Paul said. He was excited about space exploration with satellites and Sputniks being launched by us and the Russians. His winning science fair entry had been about traveling through the solar system.

"But there's no gravity on the moon," I said. "Lucky for us, there's plenty on the beach or we'd drown in all the sand flying around.

"Has anyone ever drowned in sand?" Larry, eight and the youngest, asked in an anxious voice.

Barbara turned around to him and said, "Ellen's just kidding, Larry." She had warned me about Larry's nightmares and that she was the only one who could get him back to sleep. Now I had given him a new fear to chase him through his dreams.

"What's gravity?" asked Egg, who had gotten his name when Larry had not been able to say, "Greg."

"The force that anchors us to the earth, so we don't float away." For Larry's sake, I added, "Nothing to be afraid of. Gravity is our friend."

Paul's eyes raked me. As the family science expert, he did not appreciate being usurped.

Suddenly between the dunes, the glorious white-capped Atlantic appeared. All heads turned to it.

Although I made frequent trips to the beach, the first sight of it always gave me pause.

Once she faced front again, Barbara's expression turned sullen. After her mother refused to let her stay home from this vacation, she had to quit her job at Court Street Collections, a job her parents did not know about.

As the war in Vietnam heated up, our town of Jacksonville, North Carolina, overflowed with recruits from Camp LeJeune. Local businessmen encouraged these young men, some still teenagers, to buy on credit. When they couldn't pay, the businesses set collection agencies on them.

Barbara's job had been to call a serviceman's home, pretend to be a girlfriend he'd met in Jacksonville, and try to get the man's forwarding address. Last week she told me about calling Mississippi and talking to a man's mother, who said, "I don't know any good way to tell you dear, but Bobby was killed over there three days ago." Barbara hung up in tears.

I was glad she quit.

Sergeant Novak slowed the car and turned into a cottage perched over a dune. The small pier attached to it extended into the sea like a tiny finger pointing at the horizon. This was the edge of the world, the intersection of sea and sand, sky rushing down to meet both.

After we got out of the car, the commandant called, "I have an announcement."

I fell in with the Novak troops.

"No one leaves the cottage at night. As soon as it gets dark, we stay inside. Understood?"

When no one spoke, I asked, "Why, sir?"

He stepped closer and bowed his head as if to share a secret. "Military maneuvers on the beach."

War games. According to the newspaper, our beaches and humidity replicated Vietnam's. This was the perfect place to simulate war.

"Would they shoot us?" Larry asked.

All of us reassured him that they were only playing.

That night Barbara and I were reading when Larry came in. "I'm afraid of the men in the dunes." His bottom lip trembled. "Can I sleep with you?"

We could hear the distant boom of their guns. I knew better than to tell him not to be afraid.

Barbara put an arm around him. "How about if I stay

with you until you're asleep?"

Constant wind buffeted the cottage from above. From below I could hear the high tide flowing around the cottage's pilings. The salty air, the wind, and the sound of the waves rocked me asleep waiting for Barbara's return.

Before dawn the next day Larry and Egg appeared beside our beds, dressed in shorts and holding sand pails. "You promised," Larry whispered to Barbara, so we threw on clothes and ran down to the beach with them just as the sun was pushing up from beneath the sea.

Washed by the high tide, the sand wore a stiff shell, which we broke with our feet. "Look," Egg called, running toward something he spied in the dunes. The sun glinted off a piece of metal.

"Don't," I screamed just as he dug it out of the sand. A dark thought: what if it was a bomb, a land mine, a hand grenade?

"Pound cake," he yelled, holding the tin high in triumph.

We gathered around him.

"The Marines left it behind," Barbara said. "Maybe they left other stuff, too."

But since I had screamed *don't*, they looked to me for permission.

For a moment I studied the strand and cottage not far away.

This was early in the war, before Tet, before My Lai, before Kent State. I still trusted my government. Dad told me about the domino theory, that we were in Southeast Asia to save the Vietnamese from communism. Surely the Marines would not leave things in the dunes that would harm civilians.

"Treasure hunt," I yelled.

We did make a rule that Barbara or I would pick everything up first, but this got lost in our excitement as we combed the dunes for goodies. We called to each other when we found tiny rolls of toilet paper, tins of jam, Band-Aids, iodine. Later, in the valley of the dunes, we admired our finds.

"Let's open some," Egg said, holding the tiny key at the bottom of a tin.

From the pier, Mrs. Novak called, "Children, breakfast!"

"No," Barbara whispered. "This is our secret. We tell

no one."

Larry's eyes grew large. "We'll have a secret club."

So, we hid our booty under the cottage.

Every morning thereafter the Cape Carteret Pirates Club searched the beach for goodies. In the afternoons when Mr. and Mrs. Novak left for grocery shopping, we brought out our treasures and had a feast or played hospital with the medical supplies.

I found our club's name fitting because Mrs. Novak's maiden name was Teach. She and her brood descended from Edward Teach, a.k.a. Blackbeard, the notorious pirate who'd preyed on ships traveling the eastern seaboard during colonial times.

But instead of robbing ships for treasure, we discovered ours in the dunes.

On Tuesday evening, Larry came into our bedroom, his eyes lit with excitement. "Wonder what they'll leave us tonight?" He no longer begged Barbara to stay with him until he fell asleep. The men in the dunes had become Santas.

She laughed. We felt close to the men now and talked about them often. "They're not much older than the guys at school," I told Barbara, who listed the recent graduates who had been drafted. I didn't know any of them, but Barbara was popular. She seemed to know everyone, especially the guys.

My thoughts returned to the men in the dunes. "Soon they won't be just playing war."

That night I dreamed television images of Buddhists monks in flames, helicopters flying over burning jungles, body bags. I woke in the middle of the night, my arm stretched toward the dunes as if to get their attention, perhaps to tell them: *stop*.

On Thursday, we found tins of spam, which we fried in margarine as soon as the Novaks left. The smell brought Paul into the kitchen.

He nodded at the pink slices crackling in the pan. "That stuff could be left over from the Korean War, you know." He made this appeal to me, although he never joined us, he never told on us either.

After cutting the spam into tiny squares, Barbara put it on the table, where we speared it with toothpicks and dipped it in mustard.

Yelping with delight, the little boys tried to eat it

faster than each other.

I looked at Paul. "I don't care if it's from the Revolutionary War, it's yummy. Have some."

Paul hesitated.

Suddenly I understood his burden. He had to be the family star, which Barbara could never be, while the little boys were too young. All their parents' hopes resided in Paul.

Still, he sat, speared a chunk, and ate. "For the sake of experimentation," he said and speared another.

Our last morning, we found nothing in the dunes. Disappointed, we crossed the road.

"I don't want to go in there," Barbara said of the dense jungle trees and brush beside the sound. This terrain seemed more like the Vietnam we saw on television.

But the boys begged, so eventually we agreed. Barefoot we found walking wasn't easy. After we came to the soupy marshes that edged the sound, we doubled back to the road. Along the way we found some bullet casings.

"Don't touch them," Barbara said, but when she

turned away, Egg scooped them up.

Instead of our usual breakfast of cereal that day we had eggs and bacon. After we finished eating. The commandant said, "Stay at the table a minute, kids."

Everyone sat.

Over the course of the week, the commandant's skin had tanned and the creases in his forehead smoothed. I took in the brown faces gathered around the table and realized that the beach had healed us all a little. As it would heal me again and again over the course of my life.

When things go wrong for me—my own dad's death, divorce, job disappointments—I make my way to the ocean. I find peace where sea, sand, and sky meet, a peace that goes beyond religion.

When I remember that day with the Novaks, I see their tanned happy faces around the table in the moment before their world began to change.

"I need to tell you…" their father said. "I've gotten orders to go overseas in September."

"Vietnam?" Barbara asked.

He nodded.

Later I helped Mrs. N. pack up the dishes while Paul played Chutes and Ladders with the boys.

I looked out the window to the pier. Barbara and her dad sat on the end of it, his arm around her shoulders, their heads bent toward each other.

And behind them, the wide blue Atlantic stretched across the horizon like arms holding us all.

Ellen Herbert

Ellen Herbert is the author of the novel, The Last Government Girl, winner of the Maryland Writer's Prize for Best Novel and published by AH Loyola Press. Her writing has appeared in The Washington Post, the Sonora Review, Thema, and other publications. One of her short stories was read on National Public Radio. She is a creative nonfiction editor for the international on-line zine, Halfway Down the Stairs.

Blank Page
By George Koyl

The envelope and blank piece of paper sat untouched on the table for two days now. A Kroger flier partially covered the paper. A coffee cup was just left of the envelope.

Bill Morris stepped into the kitchen and placed his lit cigarette in the corner groove on the ashtray. Bill knew that his daughter Mary had a secret sorrow. She believed that since her mother had passed twelve years ago, her dad was committing slow suicide, and he wasn't entirely sure she was wrong.

Maybe I am, he thought. He picked up the slow burning cigarette and drew deeply as he stared hard at the blank page. The envelope was addressed to Billy Morris, 721 Hiltergard Road, Davisburg, MI. No return address.

When he had pulled it from the mailbox two days ago it was buried in other mail from the ASPCA, St. Jude, and two political mailers, which all wanted money. Bill knew that this barrage of organizations and individuals holding their hands out was his own fault because of donations in the past. He assumed the envelope with the unverifiable return address was another politician and, right up to the time he was holding the envelope above the waste basket, he planned to toss it. Instead, the lack of a return address created a mystery for him. He began a guessing game. Politician? Political organization? Maybe the township office sending out an autumn flier.

Two days ago, his lips pressed together in a small smile as he slipped an index finger beneath the raised corner of the envelope where the glue hadn't taken hold. His knuckle split the top edge of the envelope in short rabbit hops, opening it bit by bit. He seized the paper inside and pulled it free, dropping the ruined envelope on the table and shaking the tri-folded paper open.

A blank page.

What the hell? He chuckled to himself, convinced it was Jamison Dirkle down at the township office. Bill took the envelope in his hand, certain the Davisburg postal mark would confirm his guess of Mr. Dirkle, but instead of Davisburg it read:

Glennie

Sep

5

Michigan

Mailed on Monday, received on Wednesday. Now, on Friday, still a mystery.

The cigarette sizzled down to the filter while resting on the ashtray. The ash curled forgotten towards the glass bottom. As hard as he tried, he couldn't recall knowing anyone in Glennie.

Bill moved the ashtray to the counter beside the sink, lighting another cigarette as he drew water to wash his breakfast dishes. Standing before the running water, he looked out his window and the lawn beyond. An obscure thought trickled into his brain, a memory forgotten long ago. He turned off the faucet.

Ahhhh. . . the thought materialized like steamy condensation evaporating off the mirror of his memory. The thick white paint of a baseboard and door casing. The burning finger of a joint. The long-ago apartment in Ann Arbor, a lifetime away. Actually, now at 72, it was more like two life-times away.

He spun around to stare hard at the blank page on the tabletop.

***

1969: He held the door for Beth, both drenched by the onslaught of the storm while walking the twelve blocks from the Michigan Theater. They had watched a one night showing of *An Affair to Remember*, a movie Beth proclaimed the most romantic movie of all time. Bill found his papers and began rolling a joint while Beth changed into dry clothes. He became irritated as she went on and on about the movie, how in the movie Nickie and Terry met on an ocean voyage and promised to meet exactly six months later at the top of the Empire State Building. A meeting that never happened. Mostly though, his irritation focused on his wet sleeve dripping water onto the cigarette papers until he had to shuttle the shreds and stems onto a new paper. As his tongue ran along the seam of the joint, he told her that he would have written the story differently.

Beth hopped onto the bed in the far corner, legs crooked into a butterfly position, her braided brown hair still wet and tied with leather strung with beads falling over her shoulders. "So, what would you do, Billy?"

A quick twist of the joint sealed it and he ripped a cardboard match free, lighting the joint and drawing THC infused smoke in deeply, holding it. When he spoke, errant puffs of smoke escaped his lips.

"Eh - a blank sheet of paper."

Beth reached for the joint and Bill held it just beyond her reach, smiling. The somber look on her face made him relent and pass the joint carefully to her. He let the rest of the smoke escape in a rushing exhale. As she drew on the joint, the end flaring in an ember red, she regarded him, her eyebrows raised.

"Nothing to chance," he said, the pleasant buzz sliding around his head, seeping down through his body. "See, this guy Nick wants to..."

"Nickie," Beth corrected him through tight lips, holding as much of the smoke in as possible.

"Yeah. Whatever. So rather than set a one and done time, he should have agreed to something more elaborate that couldn't be messed up by a stupid traffic accident."

"She was paralyzed."

"Right. Right. But see, he wants to get together with her, so he sends her a blank sheet of paper. Now, she can respond or not. Maybe she's married. Maybe she's living with a guy. Maybe she just wants this idiot out of her life."

Beth let the smoke drift slowly out as she shook her head and rolled her eyes. "Then what?"

"Uh. . . okay. Okay. So, she sends a menu from a restaurant where they will meet. Then he sends back a calendar page with a day circled and a time written in." He gestured for the joint. Beth passed it to him with no hesitation or taunting game of keep-away.

Bill studied the smoldering tip of the joint. "Yeah. Yeah. I should do that for my creative writing."

He began sucking on the end of the joint as Beth laughed, "Don't bother, Billy. That's a bird that won't fly."

The memory of Beth came rushing back like a movie freshly seen. Bill Morris started to turn back towards the sink and then wheeled back to look at the blank sheet of paper on his kitchen table and suddenly knew.

The breakup, he supposed, wasn't really a breakup.

Not the fury of a storm that crashes waves against beach rocks, pounding against a weathered dock. It was more like driftwood floating languidly in separate directions out to sea. The school year ended and Beth took a job on Mackinaw Island for the summer. Bill knew there was money in road construction and hired on with a local company out of Holly, only to break his leg before his first paycheck, dumping his Honda CB450 fishtailing on gravel just outside of town.

The phone calls, long distance and costing by the minute in those days, depleted both of their resources as the phone calls became fewer and fewer, the conversations shorter and shorter. By the time he announced he wouldn't be returning to the university because of a lack of funds, Beth, undisturbed, had promised to visit over the holidays. Then she didn't.

***

The Springfield Township Library opened its doors at 10:00 AM. 72-year-old Bill Morris was waiting when, as luck would have it, Stacie unlocked the door.

"Mr. Morris, out early today?"

"Yeah. Beautiful day. You think you can spare a few

minutes Stacie to help me?"

"Sure. What do you need?" Stacie asked, letting the set of keys slide back on the chain to the fob attached to her side.

Bill explained his dilemma, saying he was looking for an old friend, one he hadn't seen in fifty-two years, and someone whose first name was Bethany, last name Temple, but that probably had changed once or twice in the interval. Stacie led him to a computer, took a seat, logging in and asking a probing question that seemed irrelevant. "Do you know her mother or father's name?"

"Yeah, his name was Carlton and hers was Margaret, but I doubt they're still alive."

"Let's hope not." Stacie said. "You're not stalking this person, right?" Her fingers flew across the keyboard.

"At my age?" Bill asked, his face scrunching.

"Ah, here we go. Carlton Temple's obituary, Deerfield, Michigan - January 20th, 2003. Survived by his children - Bethany Mohler and husband Fred."

The fingers flew again, new screen. "Eleven Bethany Mohlers in the United States. Ah, 71-year-old Bethany Mohler, Barton City, Michigan. This may be your girl."

Bill copied down the address, "Thanks Stacie. You've been a real help - oh, wait, can you print off a menu for a restaurant in Barton City?"

"Wow, Bill. I'm starting to feel like I'm living in a Nicholas Sparks novel," She tapped enter. "That'll print at the front desk. One favor, Bill?"

"Yes?"

"I want the last page?" At his confused look, she said, "You know, how the book turns out."

He grinned.

At the post office he selected a priority mail flat-rate envelope and slipped the menu from Bob and Cassie's Diner inside. From his back pocket, he pulled out the tattered envelope with his address on it. Missive on its way for only $9.65.

The following Wednesday, another letter, this included a return address in Glennie, Michigan. His hands trembled as he took a paring knife and carefully slit the top of the envelope, leaving it whole. Inside, a page from a credit union calendar, its picture showing leaves falling along a gravel road. Friday, September 30th was circled, careful neat writing setting a time of 9:15

AM, He tucked the page back into the envelope and set it on the napkin holder where throughout the next two weeks he would stare at it during his meals.

On the scheduled date, Bill made a pot of coffee and poured his thermos full. In the refrigerator he found the two hard boiled eggs in the plastic bag he had peeled the night before. He figured three and a half hours for the trip, electing to drive US 23 along Lake Huron.

Just outside of Greenbush he checked the radio clock and saw he was going to arrive too early and, spotting a bench at a rest stop that looked across the water, he braked. A light mist fell while his canvas coat kept him comfortable. He fished the eggs from his pocket and ate these, content with the sound of tiny waves slurping against the shore.

Finally, he packed it in, tossing his trash into the bed of his pickup, hoping to arrive at Bob and Cassie's Diner by ten minutes to nine. He reached the lot at quarter to nine. Using the cap of his thermos as his cup, he poured himself coffee, barely warm enough to be enjoyable. Over the tepid liquid he studied the four cars parked on the gravel lot. The windows of the diner showed a middle-aged couple, and two tables with what appeared to be a gang of five construction guys. An eighth man was at the counter handing money to the older hostess as she passed him a thermos.

As that man stepped outside, Bill opened his door, dumped the rest of his coffee onto the gravel and started inside. He took the corner table and parked himself there. Ordering coffee, he began what felt like the longest wait in his life. There were so many questions. He had an entire menu of questions. Had she gained weight? He had. Did she color her hair? He had lost his. Did she still have that quirky sense of humor, that one that complemented his own, at least the one he had until Patty fought her predictable battle with cancer and he had interred that part of himself with her.

Across the street a car slowed, the front turn signal warning it would be pulling into the lot. From where he sat, Bill admired the sleek looking car, cherry red, and fairly new. If this was Beth, and it had to be, the time being right, she was doing okay financially. Picking up the menu, he studied the blurred words, and then pulled out his glasses.

Over the top of the menu, he watched as the car eased to the curbstone - he could see a woman - alone, at the steering wheel, waiting, waiting. His index finger twitched nervously behind the menu, and he allowed a shaky breath, a singular whispering sound escaping his lips. Had she changed? Well, of course. 72 - no, she would only be 71 years - can do that. The menu shivered as he released his other hand and covertly blew into the hollow of his palm. Cigarette and coffee breath, too late now. He continued to watch, eyes barely peering over the top of the menu.

His heart sank, emotion slithering into his stomach and coiling like a snake frozen in the early morning cold. Jesus. Beth hadn't changed at all. A little heavier, or was that just the bulky jacket? Long brown hair spilled over her shoulders. The same brown hair that had splayed over green and white pillowcases with matching sheets when they made love. The same brown hair she had tied into a ponytail at her morally mandated anti-war protests. Another soft, slow whistling of breath as his eyes glanced upwards, looking inwards and imagining the balding head with its turtleneck fringe of gray hair framing the smooth dome. His eyes dropped down to the paunch punching his polo shirt outward.

Outside, the woman walked spritely towards the door, vibrant and alive. Were those dark eyes studying the windows, questing and questioning whether she should turn around before the past suffered the ruination of reality's presence? Why the hell had he come? Disappointment, surely. Discussing who severed their singular path, forcing the diverging of their roads.

He drew a deep breath and set the menu down, ready to face his past and not at all prepared.

The door pushed open and the bell jangled.

His heart lurched and he wanted to cry. She was so young looking. Still so beautiful. She stood there, looking over the few occupied tables and then nodded to him.

"Billy?"

He snuffled. Nodded. "Beth?" He hated the sound of his voice; it was quavering and weak.

"No, Janine. Beth's daughter. Follow me."

Bill lurched unsteadily to his feet as Janice? Jenny? Janine turned and rang the bell again, not waiting. He dropped a twenty onto the table.

Janine backed the cherry red Buick out, twisting in a wide turn that carried her to the edge of the lot. Bill shuffled to his own pickup, older and with rust, pulling himself inside.

A ten-minute drive, his vehicle a few hundred feet safely behind her, before Janine slowed. The tail indicator light blinked on, and he responded in kind. This was not a house but a low-slung facility. The sign had said something about an adult assisted living center.

Something up with Beth? Broken hip? Please God, not a stroke. Not wonderful, vibrant Beth. For a moment he visited the cobweb of memory - her youthful energetic ease in making love, wrapping herself around him, pulling him into her as if melding two souls into one body. Don't panic. Remember, modern medicine was today's new God, performing little miracles all the time.

He joined Janine and together they walked toward the entrance. "I wasn't sure if I should do it," she said softly without looking at him. "Mom talked about you so much these last ten years. . ."

"The letter?"

"What? The letter? Oh, yes, she said you ruined her

favorite movie - and she loved you for it. I decided to use it because I wasn't even certain if you were the right Billy Morris, or that if you were, that you would even want to respond. Mom said it was the most romantic promise she had ever heard." Janine paused, turned her head towards him and he noticed the way the long hair fell across her shoulders.

Janine continued. "My mom loved my dad," she said fiercely, defensively. "But maybe you were her first, true love. Don't ever think she regretted loving and marrying dad; they had a great marriage. Wonderful. Still, I suppose there is always that wistful - what if -"

Bill nodded, understanding, and murmured through a tight smile, "For both of us, probably. Your mom is an incredible, amazing woman."

Janine led him inside, nodding to the receptionist and leading him down a corridor. From the open doorway of a room a woman orderly stepped out and smiled, "Your mom's waiting for you, Janny."

"Thanks Marcia. This is Billy, an old friend of hers."

Bill smiled at the word old, his heart thudding in his chest, his breathing elevated to quick, tight spurts. He started speaking as Janine turned into the room, but she stole the conversation back, "I wanted you to come early, they call it sundowner's syndrome. She's better in the morning - hey mama, I brought Billy."

The hunched form with the head bent forward stirred, iron gray hair cut short. Janine repeated his name and the head began bobbing unevenly, yoyoing up and down in unsteady movement. Brown eyes stared vacuously outward, past Bill, not seeing, focusing on a past. Withered lips parted as the head moved forward. The voice old and faltering.

"Bill - eee?"

Bill closed his eyes, squeezing his lids tight against a rush of emotion seeking tearful release. "Beth," he sighed.

George Koyl

His birth eclipsed by Sir Edmund's summit of Mt. Everest back in '53, George grew up in rural Michigan. Obtaining a B.A. in English and Masters in the Science of Administration, he worked with the Developmentally Disabled, before transferring to the Financial Institutions Bureau, and then becoming an investigator for Unemployment Insurance. Subsequently, he accepted a temporary position with the United States Forest Service in Truth or Consequences, NM, a setting he used for his Amazon Kindle science fiction trilogy Voyager.

George currently resides with his wife Terri, a college librarian, in rural Michigan where they raised their son and daughter. Terri and George have six wonderful grandchildren.

Lunch at the Sad Cafeteria
By Michail Mulvey

Our teacher, Miss Cronin, stood on a tall ladder taping our Christmas artwork to the windows of our classroom: large white snowflakes, green Christmas trees covered with colored ornaments, flying reindeer, heavenly angels with golden hair, and Santas with chubby red cheeks. Outside, the wind howled and the snow swirled. Snowflakes crashed against the windows and melted, turning into thin rivers of water, running down the glass like tears, almost.

Miss Cronin made me and Margaret hold the ladder. Big mistake. Me and Margaret hated each other. In first grade she caught me with my finger up my nose and started calling me 'Booger boy.' To get even, I called her 'Large Marge' because of her big butt and huge head.

One afternoon I told my grandmother about Margaret. I sometimes stopped off at her house after school. I knew that if she was home, she'd feed me. As I sat there at her kitchen table, devouring a boloney and cheese sandwich with mustard on rye, my grandmother told me that not only was it rude but hurtful to call people names. I loved my grandmother - especially when she fed me - so I promised never to call Margaret any rude or hurtful names ever again. I didn't promise, however, not to punch Margaret in the head if she called *me* any rude or hurtful names.

Margaret glared at me while she held one side of the ladder and I held the other. When she stuck out her tongue, I gave her the finger.

I hated Miss Cronin almost as much as I hated Margaret. I was hoping Miss Cronin would fall through the window and into the snowbank outside. Good riddance. Maybe our principal, Mrs. Tuttle, would find us a new teacher who didn't yell so much.

I didn't want Miss Cronin to die or anything, just break a couple of legs and maybe an arm so she'd have to stay home until June. Next September I'd be promoted to the third grade and I'd have a new teacher, one who maybe smiled once in a while and didn't yell so much.

I looked over at the calendar on the wall; December 20th, 1955. Only three days 'till Christmas vacation and freedom from Margaret and Miss Cronin - at least for a while.

When I looked to see if she'd taped my big snowflake to the window, I saw up Miss Cronin's skirt. She was wearing a girdle like the one I saw in my mother's laundry basket, only Miss Cronin's was huge.

"Oooo! Miss Cronin, Michael's looking up your skirt!" shouted Margaret. Miss Cronin looked down, saw me looking up her skirt and raced down the ladder. Her face was red and the veins in her neck stuck out like strands of rope.

"I was looking at the decorations," I said, cringing in fear. Speechless, Miss Cronin just glared at me. Beads of sweat began to gather on her forehead, threatening to run down her round red face.

"Liar!" yelled Margaret.

"Am not," I yelled back.

"I told you two to knock it off!" yelled Miss Cronin, grabbing us both by the arm. "I'm sick of the two of you constantly fighting. For the last time, shut up and hold the ladder steady!" Miss Cronin gave us both a long, hard look, then climbed back up the ladder, mumbling to herself all the way.

I met Margaret's parents in October, during open house. They were big. And they yelled at each other the entire time. Her father was bald and wore a shirt that was too small for his body. His yellow tie had a food stain on it and he sweat so much it looked like someone had thrown a glass of water in his face. Margaret's mother wore too much makeup and her jugs were the size of my Uncle Vinnie's head. When she walked into the classroom, everything on her jiggled.

Miss Cronin also yelled at Margaret a lot, but since she came from a family of yellers, she was probably used to it. My mother yelled a lot too. Maybe that's why my father didn't live with us anymore. I never got used to Miss Cronin's yelling, though. She made the windows rattle. Miriam Nirenstein said her teeth hurt when Miss Cronin was on a tear, which was just about every day.

Margaret had a bad temper and most times it was aimed my way because I teased her a lot. The other kids teased her too. Jimmy Vlahos called her Godzilla. I sat in the back, two seats behind Margaret. When Miss Cronin wasn't looking, I threw stuff at Margaret's head, like spit balls, gum wrappers, and other garbage. One time, when I hit her in the head with a pencil eraser, she turned around and threw her spelling book at me. She missed. Miss Cronin had a cow and sent Margaret to the office.

Margaret held the ladder and stared at me with her face all scrunched up. I was the one who should have been pissed off, she'd ratted me out for accidently looking up Miss Cronin's skirt. I let go of the ladder and tried to punch Margaret in the head. I missed and we began to wrestle.

"Booger boy!" she yelled, yanking on my hair.

"Fat ass!" I yelled, trying to kick her in the shin.

As Miss Cronin raced down, the ladder wobbled and she almost *did* fall through the window. She grabbed the two of us by the arms and started yelling, so hard spit shot out of her mouth and landed on us. I winced and tried to get away, but Miss Cronin held my arm so tight it hurt. Her fingernails were like thumb tacks.

"That's it! I've had it with the two of you!" she yelled. Margaret wiped the spit off her arm with her free hand. "Let go of me!" she yelled. Miss Cronin's eyes began to bug out even more. I was sure the two of us were headed for Mrs. Tuttle's office, but Vito Calabrese and Paul Kocak were already in there for a wet paper towel fight in the boy's lav.

Miss Cronin dragged the two of us to the cloakroom and shoved us in. "You! Over there!" she yelled at me, pointing to a corner. "And you! Over there! The two of you, sit down and shut up," she yelled. Miss Cronin glared at us for a long minute, her hands balled up in fists like she was going to punch us both out. But she just stared at us then stomped out, slamming the cloakroom door behind her.

Trying to ignore Margaret, I surveyed our jail. Along the walls of the narrow cloakroom were hooks where we hung our coats. Over the hooks was a long shelf where we placed our lunch bags and lunch boxes. Wet and muddy boots and galoshes were lined up against the walls, toes facing out. Small slushy puddles dotted the floor.

I found a dry spot and sat down, cross-legged. Margaret sat on the floor at the other end of the room, facing away from me. At first the cloak room was chilly, but when the furnace came on, warm air blew up thru the big black heat register in the floor and took the chill out of the air. I took off my wet shoes and socks and laid them on the register to dry out.

Margaret's socks were wet too, but she didn't want to put them next to mine. She pulled her coat down from the overhead hook and wrapped it around her big stinky feet.

I reached up, pulled down a heavy winter coat from one of the hooks and wrapped it around my shoulders. The nametag on the inside collar said it belonged to Jimmy Vlahos. Jimmy's mother worked part-time at Miller's Clothing Store. Unlike mine, Jimmy's coat was big and warm.

Margaret pulled down another coat, wrapped it around her shoulders and stuck out her tongue. I gave her the finger and pulled down another coat, made a cushion and sat on it. Margaret pulled down another coat, also made a cushion and sat on it. And so on, until half the coats were on the floor, piled high around us like forts. I made a pillow from one coat and lay down, my feet resting on the warm register next to my shoes and socks.

Me and Margaret did our best to ignore each other; I counted the peeling paint chips on the ceiling. Margaret picked at some crud under one of her toenails. Through the cloakroom door we could hear Miss Cronin yelling at Jimmy O'Meara. "Does she ever shut up?" I asked. "Her mouth is almost as big as yours."

"Shut up, booger boy," she whispered, flinging a piece of toe crud at me.

"No, you shut up, fat head."

I looked out the window at the far end of the room. The snow had stopped. Purple clouds raced across a gray sky. I was wishing I could hop on one and race away from this school . . . and Miss Cronin . . . and Margaret. For a moment I thought about climbing out the window and running home where I could sit in front of the TV and watch *The Lone Ranger* or *Laurel and Hardy* or *The Three Stooges* – those three knuckleheads really cracked me up. I decided to stay put, though. The cloak room was warm and dry, I was surrounded by and covered with warm coats, and nobody was yelling at me.

I got yelled at one morning when the class pledged allegiance to the flag and sang *America the Beautiful*. I couldn't remember the words, so I sang the Mickey Mouse Club song instead. I had a good singing voice - if you count loud.

I got yelled at when I farted during reading one day, but I couldn't help it. My mother made me eat prunes with my cereal one morning. "These will make you regular," she told me. I wasn't sure what she meant, but I was constipated and the school nurse told my mother to feed me prunes for breakfast . . . and cabbage soup for supper. She stopped when I cut a wet fart in my sleep. Morris Molowitz said he cut a wet fart once too, but not in his sleep. It was at a family picnic one summer at Lake Wetmore. *Wetmore*. That's funny.

I got yelled at when I fell asleep at my desk one morning. I was sick the night before but my mother sent me to school anyway. "I have to go to work," she said, "and there's nobody here to watch you." I told Miss Cronin I wasn't feeling good, but she ignored me. During spelling, my head got heavy and I fell asleep at my desk. I woke up when Miss Cronin poked me with a ruler. There was a small puddle of drool where my head had been resting. Miss Cronin made me wipe it up with my sleeve, wouldn't even let me get a paper towel from the boy's lav.

When her stomach growled Margaret stood up and grabbed her lunch bag off the shelf. Before you could say 'boloney and cheese with mustard on rye,' her sandwich was gone. Just like that. She crumpled up the paper bag and threw it at me. Margaret burped then reached up and grabbed another lunch bag. Sandra Neri's name was written on the side.

"That's not your lunch," I said, throwing her crumpled lunch bag back at her. Margaret ignored me and took out a cream cheese and jelly sandwich wrapped in tinfoil. She shoved the sandwich in her face, chewing with her mouth open just to annoy me. The cream cheese stuck to her teeth. I wanted to puke.

As I watched Margaret eat, *my* stomach growled and I remembered I hadn't eaten breakfast. We were out of milk . . . and cereal. And my mother hadn't yet gotten home when I left for school, so I had no lunch either. I gave Margaret a dirty look, stood up and grabbed a Superman lunch box from the shelf. Inside was a tuna salad sandwich wrapped in wax paper. I loved tuna fish.

There was a thermos, too, but it was filled with tomato soup. I hated tomato soup.

I wolfed down the sandwich before you could say 'spaghetti and meatballs in marinara sauce.' Still hungry, I grabbed a Lone Ranger lunch box off the shelf. This one had a liverwurst sandwich, also wrapped in wax paper. I hated liverwurst, but there was chocolate milk in the thermos. I drank the chocolate milk right down. My mother tried to make me eat liverwurst once. I understood why it was called liver-'worst.' I'd rather eat cold beet soup and I hated cold beet soup. My mother had another name for cold beet soup, some funny-sounding name.

Margaret wiped her mouth on her sleeve then reached up again, this time grabbing a Hopalong Cassidy lunch box. Inside was a chicken salad sandwich. She took a sniff, then ate the whole thing in only three bites, it seemed. She also found a banana, which the big ape peeled and shoved down her cake hole.

I grabbed a greasy lunch bag off the shelf. It didn't have a name on it, but knew it probably belonged to Dominick Veneziano. Inside was a meatball grinder with provolone cheese. I picked out and ate the meatballs and provolone slices, dropping the soggy Italian bread back in the bag. I wiped my hands on the coat I was sitting on.

In one lunch bag I found a sandwich made with those stinky little fishes, the kind my Uncle Vinnie sometimes ate when he drank beer. I threw one of the little fishes at Margaret and hit her in the chest. She threw it back at me but missed. To my surprise, I found I liked mashed potato and baked bean sandwiches. I held up the bag and saw Johnny Hogan's name. Johnny's father was a cop.

In one lunch box I found a special prize, a package of Twinkies. I smiled and held one up like I was giving Margaret the middle finger. She laughed.

Margaret found a package of SnoBalls and held them out in front of her like two pink and white coconut-covered tits. She shoved one in her face, smiling as she chewed. We both found strawberry licorice. It turned out me and Margaret both liked licorice. She traded me a Charleston Chew for a Turkish Taffy and we split a box of Good 'N Plenty.

Anyway, this went on for awhile, me and Margaret trying to outdo each other, taking bites out of sandwiches, opening our mouths and showing each other the contents, spitting out what we didn't like, throwing crumpled up wax paper at each other. In no time we'd gone through most of the lunches and had eaten parts or most of several sandwiches, some of the fruit, and all the candy. Margaret sure could eat. Having missed at least two meals, I was able to keep up with her. I'd never say it to her face, but being locked in a cozy and quiet cloakroom with Margaret was better than sitting at my desk doing arithmetic while Miss Cronin yelled and spit on me.

Metal lunch boxes, brown paper lunch bags, piles of crumpled wax paper, and balls of aluminum foil littered the floor of the cloakroom. I felt a little sleepy, so I curled up on the floor inside my fort and wrapped myself with Jimmy Vlahos' big winter coat. Margaret yawned, stretched, burped, then fell over onto a coat and closed her eyes. The heat came on again and warm air filled the small room.

I must have fallen asleep because the next thing I heard was someone yelling; "What are you two doing?" I sat up and there, standing in the door of the cloakroom was Miss Cronin, holding her head in her hands and with a look on her face like someone had just run over her dog.

"I asked what you two are doing?" she yelled again. That's when I realized Margaret was lying next to me, snoring. She must have rolled over in her sleep. I hoped Miss Cronin wasn't thinking what I thought she was thinking, that Margaret and I were doing what I caught my Uncle Vinnie and Aunt Sophia doing one Sunday morning when I stayed at their house while my mother was away.

I jumped up and moved away from Margaret who was still sound asleep. She probably could have slept through a fire drill. I nudged Margaret with my foot. She snorted, sat up, looked around, and scratched her stomach.

Miss Cronin stood there, looking around at all the crumbled wax paper, banana peels, candy wrappers and other garbage. I think she wanted to scream again or yell something, but for once, nothing came out.

Since Vito Calabrese and Paul Kocak were still in the principal's office, Miss Cronin had nowhere else to send us. She dragged me and Margaret back into the classroom and sat us on the floor in separate corners at the back of the room, facing away from the class.

"Don't move. Don't say a word. Don't turn around," she warned. And she looked like she meant it, standing there with her eyes bugging out and her fists all balled up again. So, I sat there in the corner, playing with dead flies. Margaret drew stick figures in the dust with her finger.

At eleven forty-five Miss Cronin sent the class to the cloakroom for their lunches. When my classmates found all the lunch boxes and lunch bags broken into and their sandwiches eaten or bitten into, they came back ready to kill us. But Miss Cronin, hands on hips, glared at them. They all sat down at their desks and ate what we had left for them. Not much.

After twenty minutes Miss Cronin let our class outside for recess. Me and Margaret waited until all our classmates were outside, then got our coats and followed. They were waiting for us, lined up like in that John Wayne movie, *The Searchers*. Duke and his Texas Ranger buddies were riding through the desert when suddenly there's a line of Indians riding on either side, waiting to jump them.

As me and Margaret slowly walked across the playground, our hungry classmates began to gather snow with their gloves. The slushy wet snow that covered the playground was perfect for snowballs. When me and Margaret got halfway across the playground, our classmates began to pelt us.

"Booger boy," yelled Dominick Veneziano. He hit me in the side of the head with a snowball. "That's for eating my grinder!"

"I didn't eat the whole thing," I yelled back, trying to scrape snow out of my ear.

"You ate the best part, booger boy," he yelled, bending down to make another snowball.

"Fat ass," yelled others as they pelted Margaret. Jimmy Vlahos yelled something, but I could barely hear him with snow in my ear.

Dodging snowballs, chunks of ice, rocks, sticks, and anything else they could find, Margaret and me retreated to a corner of the playground, took cover behind a big tree and tossed snowballs back as fast as we could make them. I took one in the eye and another in the crotch, both thrown by Maura Fagan - I'd eaten her strawberry licorice. Miss Cronin stood in the window of our classroom screaming something, but we couldn't hear her.

Margaret took one big snowball in the chest thrown by Dan O'Connor. She'd eaten his SnoBalls. After about ten minutes, our classmates, red-faced and sweaty, backed off, lobbing rude and hurtful names instead.

Me and Margaret were both covered with wet snow. Snot ran down my nose. Margaret's face was red and she was breathing heavy. But we had beaten them off, like in *The Searchers* when Duke and his buddies fought off those Indians. My ear hurt, but we'd survived, at least for now. But who knew what they'd do to us after school, on our way home.

Margaret wiped her nose on her sleeve.

"Good arm," she said.

"Not a bad arm yourself—for a fat ass," I answered, fighting a smile.

Margaret punched me in the chest and grinned a big shit-eating grin.

For the rest of recess, we hid behind the tree and

kept an eye on our classmates at the other end of the playground. Thin white clouds raced across the sky, revealing patches of blue. The sun finally came out and reflected off our classroom windows. Miss Cronin, still standing there yelling, disappeared in the light.

Michail Mulvey

Michail Mulvey is a retired educator who taught for almost half a century, at all levels, from kindergarten to college. He holds an MFA in creative writing from Southern Connecticut State University and has had over fifty short stories published in literary magazines and journals such as Prole(UK), Johnny America, Poydras, The Front Porch Review, The Summerset Review, The Umbrella Factory, Drunk Monkeys, Roadside Fiction (IRL), Crack the Spine, Spank the Carp, and War, Literature and the Arts." In 2013 he was nominated for a Pushcart Prize.

He spends his days reading, writing, watching English Premier League Football, napping, playing with his grandchildren, and sipping Proseco on the back deck on warm summer nights.

Hamburger Girl
By Patti Ann Pecina

It was movie night. A pretty big deal at our house as it was something we didn't do too often. Seems like we'd waited forever and now Saturday night was finally here. Not so exciting in today's world, but this was Los Angeles 1967 and I was 9 years old. I could hardly wait.

I loved going to the drive-in theater snuggled in to "my section" of the station wagon with my pillow and blanket, listening to the crackly speaker hung on the window, feeling the night breeze, and enjoying the treats. And Oh! The treats! Candy, soda, and premade buttery "momcorn" with just the right amount of butter and salt. We never bought from the snack bar, "Too expensive and the lines are too long" proclaimed stepdad Ed whenever we asked. "We" consisted of my two sisters, one older than me, Penny (bossy pants), and one younger, Sharon (sassy pants), and then there was me, quiet me (fancy pants), I preferred dresses to pants.

I love my sisters now, but growing up it was not exactly "Little Women" around our house. More like little witches who fought all the time. Penny's favorite saying was, "I'm the oldest so I am the boss of you guys," and she would give us a ridiculous command we had to obey. Sharon was just plain mischievous and always getting into my things. One day she decided it might be fun to cut all the hair off my prized Barbie and her friends Midge and Skipper the day after I received them for my birthday. Ken was left out of the fray because his hair was painted on, he wouldn't grow real fake hair until years later. I came home from school and found them naked and afraid on the floor, their stiff arms sticking out as if pointing at the trash can, where at the bottom I found a tangled mess of blond hair. I cried for days; it's just not that fun to play with Barbie and friends after they've been snatched baldheaded. But I survived this terrible trauma and like I said I love my sisters now, and I'm pretty sure years ago I annoyed the heck out of them too. Back to movie night.

I will never understand why, but this movie night my mom had the bright idea of inviting the neighbor boys

Danny (Penny's age) and Donny (my age) Bigmouth to come along. Not really their last name but fitting, trust me. I'm quite sure my mom didn't grasp the thought that it might be embarrassing for us to climb into the back of the station wagon in our fuzzy PJ's holding our pillows with the known bully boys we suffered with daily at school. Or maybe she did, she could be mean sometimes. So, I clamored awkwardly into the car with my sisters not daring to look at the Bigmouth brothers, seeking a spot to call my own. Five kids crammed like sardines in the back of the station wagon with the seats down, airbag and seatbelt free, parents smoking at will. It was a very carefree and dangerous time, but somehow, we all survived.

This night was especially exciting as we were stopping for dinner before the movie at that magical place with the Golden Arches. I could hardly contain myself. We would just eat in the car and then carry on to the drive-in, that way the parents wouldn't have to repack the sardines. While Ed was taking everyone's order, my mother turned around from her seat in the front and said to me, "You'll need to get a regular burger tonight as we're running late, and we don't have time to wait for your simpleton." The P.C. Police had not yet arrived in 1967 Los Angeles and surprisingly this is what they called a plain dry burger at McDonald's for the picky eater in your home. My cheeks flushed with embarrassment as I envisioned the taunts from Danny and Donny next week at school already. Oh, dear God help me.

"Or." mom continued, "why don't you try a fish filet?" A what?? I thought to myself, but she apparently telepathically heard what I was thinking because she went on to say, "Oh come on, it tastes just like chicken, you'll like it. Now hurry up, decide, we've got to go!" Weighing my options, I just couldn't fathom having a regular hamburger with that suspicious limp pickle and smelly tiny onions in the middle, so I blurted out, "Uh okay, yes okay I'll do the fish filet." Words I regretted the moment they left my lips, because of THE RULE.

Yes, there was an etched in stone rule on movie night and there was no getting around it: YOU MUST FINISH ALL OF YOUR DINNER OR YOU WILL NOT GET ANY TREATS INCLUDING THE MOMCORN. A movie night fate worse than death. This was a particularly hard rule for picky me because I did not like anything EXCEPT a plain, dry simpleton burger. I wouldn't even eat spaghetti as a child as I didn't like "wet noodles". I still don't. Once, in an effort to get me to eat Sunday breakfast after I sat at the table staring at my plate for two agonizing hours, my exasperated mom shouted, "Eat those pancakes now or I'm going to freeze them, cut a hole in them, and you will wear them to school tomorrow as a bracelet!" Once again, she could be mean. I still have the pancake bracelet and wear it on occasion to bring me down when I am feeling too happy.

Just a side note about my mom, she was what they called a bombshell back in the day, beautiful and curvy with a true swish in her walk and a blond beehive doo. She was just as strict as she was beautiful and it was a rare day that you could pull one over on her. No nonsense in mom style, she never just said no when we asked for something expensive; her final and stock answer always was,"Well, you can wish in one hand and poop in the other because you're not going to get it!" She was also crafty and a good cook (I realized that later when I finally ate something) with a complete meal on the table every night and a remedy for whatever ailed you. If you could mix Marilyn Monroe, with a spoonful of Mary Poppins, a dash of Betty Crocker and then fold in a very large cup of Miss Hannigan, you'd have my mom. She could beat the crap out of Moms of today.

So, there I sat regretting my decision in the station wagon, in the parking lot, under the Golden Arches waiting for Ed to return with our dinner. This surprise impending change in my regular diet had thrown me into a tailspin. I looked out the window and desperately searched the front of the McDonald's for Ed's position in line. You see back in the day (and what may seem like the stone age to some of you reading this), there were no dining rooms and no drive-throughs at McDonald's, just a few walk-up order windows and outdoor cement tables. I finally spotted him standing with the rest of the impatient dads checking his watch every few seconds and glancing back at the car. He was next in line so I'd better hurry! Just as I was ready to open the door and run screaming through the parking lot "Wait! I don't want a fish filet, just give me the weird burger" he turned to look at the car again and locked eyes with me. I gasped and slid back so he couldn't see me, but I swear I heard his voice say, "Don't even think of it young lady, you made your choice and you're going to eat and like every bit of it!"

Why didn't I cry, throw a tantrum and demand a plain, dry burger? Because it wouldn't have worked with my mom or Ed, and I wasn't that child anyway. I was the obedient one who did what she was told. The obedient one who was about to do the most shocking thing she'd ever done in all her nine years.

When the sandwich wrapped in light green paper arrived, I opened it and took one whiff of the stinky fish and knew: I. Cannot. Eat. This. What in the world am I going to do? From where I sat, I could smell the momcorn and see the treat bag on the front seat floor and as I stared longingly at it, I could feel the tears welling up in my eyes. I've got to do something I thought as I nibbled on my French fries. Glancing nervously around the car, I noticed that no one was paying the slightest attention to me, it was as though I was invisible. Chubby Danny and Donny were busy inhaling their burgers, my parents were chatting in the front seat, and my sisters were trying to enjoy their food in their uncomfortable PJ's. So invisible me seized the moment. In my glance around, I noted that the window I conveniently was sitting next to was open just enough to slide a fish filet through and … That's. What. I. Did. Pushing it out quickly, I said a silent prayer in hopes that the hundreds of birds that regularly congregate in fast food parking lots would immediately find it on the pavement, pick it up and carry it away forever. Once the offending filet left my hand, I glanced around rather guiltily this time and again, no one noticed me. It is good to be invisible sometimes.

Just as I breathed a sigh of great relief, my mom turned around, looked at the empty fish filet wrapper for a long time and finally said, "Wow!" so loud that I about jumped out of my skin. And then a little softer, "I can't believe you ate that. Now we know what we can order for you next time!" "Um uh huh" I managed to whisper. "But I still really like the plain hamburger. This fish filet has kind of given me an upset stomach." Reaching up to touch my nose, I wondered how long it would take for it to resemble Pinocchio's for the giant lie I just told. "Oh no" she said sympathetically, "well, you don't have to eat those fries if you don't want to, give them to Danny and Donny to finish off." Sure, why not, I thought – now I will have plenty of room for all the treats.

As everyone finished their meals and collected the trash for Ed to dispose of, I held my breath as he stepped out of the car to walk to the receptacle. If the birds hadn't done their job, then I am a dead not-so-obedient-invisible-girl. But Ed jumped back into the car, put the keys in the ignition and turned on the motor. I believe I am in the clear! A feeling of great relief and happiness enveloped me.

The car was now backing out of the parking lot, and we were on our way. But just when I was starting to relax, one of the Bigmouth brothers (probably Danny) yells out, "Hey there's a hamburger stuck on our car!" The other Bigmouth chimed in, "That's not a hamburger, that's a fish filet!" Uh oh…the darn thing was sitting perfectly on the outside door handle, bun lid and all as if it had just been cooked and gently placed there by Ronald McDonald himself. As a reminder to anyone younger than me reading this, in those days car door handles stuck out about 2 to 3 inches from the door itself for easy opening and catching errant sandwiches.

As you can imagine, I was no longer invisible and all eyes were on me now, especially my mom's and they were effectively burning a hole right through me. Yes, if looks could kill, I would not be writing this at present. I sat frozen waiting to hear my punishment and I knew it would be BIG. Especially since, *Thou shall not waste even a crumb of food,* was the 11th commandment at our house. I learned this life lesson with the bracelet incident and the time I gave the last Sunday donut to our dog, Bridgette, whose mournful eyes were most definitely telling me, "Please, I really neeeeeed that donut." I received five quick lashes on my b-u-t-t from Ed's leather belt for that little food waste crime and it was #1 on my list of sins to confess to Father O'Malley the following week. When I did, I think I heard him laugh through the confessional.

The entire car fell silent as I waited for my punishment. Would it be extra chores? A month's restriction? Another lashing from Ed? I waited what seemed like an eternity and she finally spoke, "You get no treats tonight!" And with that she turned back to Ed and said, "Let's get going, we'll miss the beginning of the movie." Wait - that is it?? I already knew that the treats were non-negotiable but what else? This did not seem right. There just HAD to be more. My mother was *never* light on punishment and actually had several wooden spoons strategically laid out around the house to remind us of our fate if we misbehaved. Of course, I was very upset that I had to watch everyone else indulge in those great treats especially since I was kind of hungry having eaten no dinner, but surely this fish filet offence warranted a much bigger punishment. What was my mom up to here? Why isn't she telling me what a terrible child I am especially with all the starving children in the world? As I deeply pondered this, I decided to punish myself and I put my head down on my pillow, covered it with my blanket and quietly sobbed to sleep. There would be no treats AND no movie for me this night.

The rest of the weekend I waited and waited for my real punishment, and it never came. Back at school on Monday, I found out what my punishment was to be. Danny and Donny Bigmouth wasted no time in telling every child at St. Jerome's Parochial School all about it.

Even my favorite teacher, Sister Mary Joseph knew and she could barely keep a straight face when she looked at me. Every child who passed me felt the need to scream out "Hamburger Girl" and then "That's not a hamburger, that's a fish filet!" followed with loud bouts of laughter. For all I know, my mom paid them an annual salary to taunt me for a year. And it really hurt when my best friend, Jane Fisher got in on the action. I did not speak to her for two weeks until the day she showed up at my house with her beautiful hair intact Barbie's as a peace offering. I really couldn't resist that. I suffered for months through the relentless taunting, and it seemed everyone knew what a food sinner I was. I half expected Father O'Malley to make me serve my penance by wearing a McDonald's employee uniform to school instead of the regulation plaid jumper.

I prayed each week for Friday to arrive quickly so I could have some peace at home on the weekend and not be constantly reminded of my terrible deed. Even my sisters had tired of the whole episode and Penny had started telling kids at school to knock it off and leave me alone. It was fitting since she's really the only one allowed to ridicule me as my sisterly boss.

Finally, one Saturday I was in the backyard with my dog Bridgette, my only true friend and lover of donuts, when I heard a noise from the back fence. As fate would have it, we happened to share this fence with the Bigmouth family as they lived around the block, directly behind us. I looked up and there they were, Danny and Donny perched high on the fence looking down on me and the taunting began once again. Geesh, I thought, do these two bobo heads ever stop? I just sat there unable to move as Bridgette started to bark and their voices got louder and louder. And then, out of nowhere there was a blast of water squirting the boys nearly off their perch and then two sets of hands swooping me up and out of the way. My sisters had come to my rescue and were dragging me back to the house and into my mom's arms who hugged me hard. My heart beat with love for my family.

Looking behind me I saw the source of the water. It was Ed with the garden hose at full blast and he never looked angrier. "You two boys think it's funny to pick on a girl?" he screamed at them. One of them mimicked him and got a quick shot of water to the face. "What did you say son?" "Nothing sir," a dripping Danny said quickly. "Well good then" Ed continued "If I find out that either one of you is bothering her in any way shape or form, I'm coming over to pay you and your parents a little visit, understood?" "Yes sir" they both said as they scrambled down their side of the fence and ran off. And that was that, my food sin penance was complete.

Back at school I was once again happily invisible; the Bigmouth brothers left me alone and soon after that they moved away when their father changed jobs. I often wonder what became of them and in what prison they now reside.

As for myself, I still hate fish filets, in fact I hate all fish – which could quite possibly be psychological. As irony would have it, my first real job at 16 years old was at McDonald's where I spent two years learning the fascinating fast-food ropes including the stinky fish filet fry station. I must have done a good job because I was promoted to Crew Chief and got a few small raises in pay along the way. Even after my movie night food sin trauma, I harbor no ill will towards McDonald's, in fact, I thank them for setting the template for the strong work ethic that I carry with me to this day. My supervisor did ask me if I wanted to go into management, but I thoughtfully declined as I knew I had bigger fish to throw out the window.

Patti Ann Pecina

Patti is a native Southern Californian and currently resides with two wild and crazy but adorable rescue pups, Norman and Stevie. She is over the moon that her story "Hamburger Girl" has been selected to be published in this year's "Stories Through the Ages Baby Boomers Plus" book. She wishes she could time travel back to 1967 and tell her 9-year-old self, "Don't worry your humiliating food sin story will one day be shared with many and hopefully bring laughter to all who read it."

After 20 years as a business owner in restaurant recruiting, she thought she might retire and enjoy the good life, but a nonprofit that teaches culinary training to at risk youth had other ideas and hired her as their Dean of Students, the most rewarding opportunity she has ever been blessed to have.

She has always used her imagination to fuel creative endeavors, whether it's thinking outside the box in her own business or being crafty with clay or sewing to fulfill her creative heart.

She loves visiting Oregon and the special people who live there, her daughter Kelli, son in law, Nick, and her adorable and talented grandson Luca who is thrilled that the story he asks her to tell him over and over has now been published.

Dirge
By Susan M. Pomerantz

Giant weeping willows whipped themselves into a symphony; silhouettes against the October sky. Kendra tasted the storm in the suddenly menacing air, as she struggled with her basket of the few remaining apples. She made it to the far barn just as the first of the lightning fractured the charcoal skies.

"I'm keeping you company 'til this passes, Betty," she confided in the big cow. "Don't be afraid, Barney," she murmured, stepping into the stall to embrace Betty's restless calf.

Jake, his burr-riddled tail curled between his legs, sought comfort at Kendra's feet. Papa would see the lantern light and know she was safe. He would keep her supper for her, and besides, she was expert at eating around wormholes and rot spots in apples. It was nice leaving the night's care and feeding of her brothers and sisters to Papa. There was rarely a chance to sit and read or pick up her recorder, even though she had more time since Momma died. Her two-year-old plastic recorder from fifth grade was hidden in the place where the beams met above Betty's stall. The storm would give her an hour to let her breath pass any way it wanted out through the recorder.

Kendra reached up for her recorder and down fell her copy of *A Tree Grows in Brooklyn*. She'd borrowed the book from the library and loved it so much that she hid it so she wouldn't have to return it. She felt guilty, but was saving her allowance for six months to be able to pay the library. Momma and Papa never allowed such extravagances as buying a book. She had misgivings about her mendacity but maybe, in a twisted way, justified because she had a way to name this dishonesty that was better than simply calling it a lie. Words were Kendra's truest companions.

She mouthed the words *aperture* and *embouchure* as she brushed the dust away and put the recorder to her lips.

Momma never understood why Kendra needed to read a book more than once, anyway. Truth be told,

Momma looked askance at her eldest child for reading anything at all except for books she had to read for school. About all they shared, brooded Kendra, was their wild red hair.

For a while before the end, when Momma looked at her, at any of them, it was askance. No, no. That wasn't it. It was more like she was looking through them. She smiled on occasion, but the sparkle had gone from her eyes. Momma was looking at but not seeing Kendra, Papa, the little ones, not even baby Carl. Looking at but not seeing the potatoes she expertly peeled. Looking at but not seeing herself in the mirror as she brushed her hair. Then she stopped brushing her hair much at all.

But Papa understood about books. He was the one to read to them. Coming in smelling rankly of the fields and the barn, of diesel and tractor exhaust, he'd collect the small ones on his lap, even on Momma's worst days, wet diapers and snotty noses and all, and read to them. The consonants and vowels of the brothers Grimm flew from the tattered pages, lining the nests of their childhood dreams.

Kendra took over for Papa when she got big enough

to hold the babies and read into the tops of their sleepy heads. This gave Papa a chance to wash up and take his cold Schlitz from the fridge before he joined them on the couch, stray water droplets glistening from his whiskers.

When Momma would look in, Kendra would be torn. She'd wander out to help Momma with supper and then back in to help Papa with the kids. By the time seventh grade came around though, supper duties fell entirely to Kendra. Papa never got cross with Momma even though the only thing that ever made Papa speak even the slightest bit sharply was if they were sitting around when there was work to be done.

Momma spent most days just sitting and looking out the bay window, out over the road, like she was expecting someone. Papa would come in, bend his six-foot frame at the waist, kiss Momma's head, and brush wisps of hair back from her face. He would whisper her name. If only Papa's magic could break the spell.

"Rose. Rose, honey. Here's your pill." He'd hand her a glass of cool water and watch as she dutifully swallowed. She'd dig up a smile for him, on better days, and hand him back the glass. On better days.

Aunt May came one day in July, which upset Kendra in some inscrutable way. She lived all the way in San Francisco, California. *San-fran-cisco-cal-i-for-nia.* They saw her at Christmastimes, but here she'd come out in the summer to help. Aunt May joked with Papa that, yes, she remembered how to tend a Vermont farm.

She and Momma were twins in birthday and red hair only, they would always joke. When Aunt May was just eighteen, the year Kendra was born, she escaped to the city as soon as she scraped up enough to buy a bus ticket.

"Kendra, honey," began Aunt May as she stood at the counter drying the last of the supper dishes. Kendra was twirling around, modeling the dress Aunt May brought her.

"I love it, Auntie. I simply love it!" Kendra threw her arms around her aunt's waist.

"Kendra." Aunt May turned and held her by shoulders at a gentle arm's length. "Tomorrow, your Papa and I are taking Momma to a hospital."

Kendra whispered, "No. She's been better since you got here." Aunt May didn't see that since she had come, Momma washed up. She dressed. She even smiled and laughed a little while they were setting the table.

"Well, she needs to go just for a little while. We're leaving before dawn so go on in and say good night."

Kendra could see the willows from the dormer window in the cozy attic bedroom Papa made for her. The heat of the day hovered, unimpressed by the box fan. The distant willow fronds hung like a sheet of arpeggios against the moonlight. Kendra's mind turned and whirred with the fan blades. An instinct was lurking.

What was it Momma had said? *I love you, too, Kendra.* She hadn't said that in a long time. Then, *You know where the school clothes are stored,* but why would Kendra need to know that? Momma would surely be back before the summer was out.

Kendra tried later to remember whether she sprang up to run downstairs before or after the shotgun blast tore the night open.

There was confusion in the kitchen as Papa and Aunt May fell over each other to get out the back door, still open. Momma never made it past the side yard. She was on the ground laying partly over the gun. Something was really wrong where her head should be. Kendra turned away from the scene and looked instead at the towels still on the line. How could she forget to bring them in! She began babbling about the towels, grabbing them off the line, clothespins flying everywhere, Aunt May pulling her away. The gorge rising in Kendra's throat over little bits of Momma's insides sticking to the terry cloth would repeat for a very long time.

The Fords and the Gowens came when they saw the police lights over the hill. Mrs. Ford and Mrs. Gowen guided Kendra back toward the house where her brothers and sisters were mercifully still asleep. Mr. Ford and Mr. Gowen seemed half of Papa's height, their hands reaching up to Papa's shoulders. Papa held his head in his hands. For a second, Kendra saw Momma where Aunt May stood—thought that Momma had just got up right there. Had just enough of the commotion and just got up. Policemen and the ambulance squad workers moved in choppy slow motion against the lights that flashed red to blue, red to blue.

Through the rest of the summer, Kendra pretended not to notice that Papa was packing up the house. The beginning of eighth grade was so busy, she put everything else out of mind.

Sleet pelted the barn roof, and Betty, doing her part to contribute to the concert, was lowing while Kendra played her variations on Pachelbel's Canon. Kendra had not noticed that the lightning subsided until Jake's tail started thwacking when Papa slid the door open. He wiped sleet from his beard and tousled Kendra's hair. "Bring those things into the house, darlin', and pack them in your suitcase." He walked into Betty's stall and hugged her hard around the neck, burying his face in her shoulder, smacking her flank firmly, like he wanted to take the scent and feel of her with him. He scratched Barney's soft black fur just behind his ear where it blended with the white fur. He cleared his throat.

"You be a good girl for the Gowens, Betty. You've been a good, good girl." He knelt beside Jake and rubbed behind both ears at the same time. "You take good care of 'em, Jake, boy. Good, good boy." He could say no more.

Papa piled them all into the station wagon the next morning. He'd been saving some mail that Aunt May had sent Kendra to give to her when they left. It was a thick envelope with a long letter that Kendra would save to read. She thumbed through the polaroids of her new room, a piano in their new living room, the neighborhood with houses all close together, the library, her new school. There was even one of her new teacher, Mr. Bouchard. She'd never had a man teacher before. Papa said this was an adventure for all of them. She tried to feel excited.

"Bye-bye, house," came a tiny voice from the way-back seat. Then, "Bye-bye, Momma."

Kendra peered out at the sun coming up over the meadow, making weak halos around the swaying willows as they conducted their never-ending dirge. They had shed their last leaves, bereft already of the family. *Bereft.* The word syncopated with the rumble of tires all the way west.

Susan M. Pomerantz

About to retire from over three decades of teaching (college sociology and high school English), Susan Pomerantz is ready to enjoy a full-time life of writing and reading voluminously, yoga, gardening, chatting with friends in her zen garden, traveling, taking long walks, and maybe picking up the piano again. She and her husband, Steve, are happy to live in beautiful South Jersey, and to have their two fantastic thirty-something children living close enough by in Philadelphia. Going into the city is a chance to visit them and visiting them is a chance to go into the city!

Susan has been writing stories since the days when she was tasting the colorful, deliciously-named crayons as well as using them to form words. Since then, she has had some of her stories published in literary magazines. She is ready to publish her first novel and is knee-deep so far in writing her second novel.

Killer at Kozy Kove Kampground
By Thom Schilling

In a few hours we'd be shrouded in darkness. We had driven four hundred miles since leaving home and the endless hours in a station wagon with four preteen children were taking a toll. With each mile I was barraged with repeated complaints: "Mom, he's touching me!" or "Move over!" or "Dad, I need to go to the bathroom," and the constant repetition of the most annoying question on any road trip, "Are we there yet?"

I relished the thought of stopping for the night.

We were taking a family vacation on a tight budget. That meant we loaded 1,000 pounds of gear into our 1977 Oldsmobile Custom Cruiser Station Wagon and embarked on a driving and camping expedition across the southeastern United States. If there was an upside to our trip, the children's school let out a week before the other schools in America. We had our pick of the best campsites at the best campgrounds. All parks would be litter free and tidy, with the smell of fresh paint. Yes, for once we would stay at a park that looked *exactly* like those in travel brochures.

Anxious from sitting in the car, the kids needed to be set free so they could burn-off their endless energy. Consequently, they were becoming more creative and more obnoxious. My wife, Barbara, reached her limits of vacation frustration about the same time the children started to play, 'Guess That Road-Kill,' a game they invented whereby they took turns trying to identify the furry little waffles of flattened critters lying on the roadside.

Finally, Barbara pleaded, "Honey, isn't it about time to stop for the night?"

Like a maniac on a mission, I was hell-bent on driving as many miles as I could before dark, but I knew she was right. I held off stopping as long as I could but the words, "Where do you want to stop?" escaped my lips.

"I don't know. Where do *you* want to stop?" challenged my wife.

For the next fifteen minutes we volleyed the phrase,

"Where do you want to stop?" until finally I snarled, "I've had it! We're staying at the next campground we come to!"

Silence blanketed the car for several awkward moments, until we saw the sign next to the interstate: KOZY KOVE KAMPGROUND NEXT EXIT.

Taking a deep breath, I grunted, "Well? What do you think?"

Short on patience, Barb responded with a menacing, "FINE!"

The kids cheered as we pulled off the highway. The sign posted at the end of the exit ramp had a large red arrow with twelve inch tall words - KOZY KOVE KAMPGROUND, THIS WAY!

We turned on a four-lane road and drove for several miles. The road narrowed to two lanes for a few miles and then the pavement ended. We drove another mile on a dirt trail before we saw the next sign. YOU'RE NOT LOST. KOZY KOVE KAMPGROUND IS JUST AHEAD!

My wife exhaled loudly. "I don't know. Are you sure you want to go there?"

By this point I was committed. Our search for the

Holy Grail of campgrounds was at hand. I forced a tired smile to my face. "It'll be okay. They've located the campground off the highway and put it back in the woods so we won't have to hear the trucks running up and down the interstate all night."

Barb exhaled deeply. "I suppose, but I've got a funny feeling about this place."

I patted her knee reassuringly as I drove up the trail, but secretly I wondered if we were doing the right thing. A few minutes later we started up a long hill; just before the crest there was another sign. GOOSE IT! YOU'RE ALMOST THERE! KOZY KOVE KAMPGROUND JUST AHEAD!

"Goose it?" quizzed my wife.

Before I could respond my oldest son shouted, "Hey, look at that!"

As we topped the hill, we saw a man wearing tattered bib overalls and a large straw hat. He raised his double barrel shotgun over his head and hollered something in Carolinian gibberish. Although I couldn't understand one word, I nodded and waved as we passed. Every other set of eyes in the car locked on him.

Once again Barb echoed, "I've got a funny feeling about this place."

With all of the conviction and credibility of a '70s used car salesman, I reasoned, "Honey, that's just how they say 'hello' in rural South Carolina. There's nothing to worry about."

Suddenly the children all yelled, "We're here!"

I pulled into the campground and parked in front of the general store. The doors to the car opened and our four kids ran in four directions. Before I could get out of the car my spouse said, "Look! There isn't anyone else in the campground. Do you think they're open?"

"The door to the general store is open. I'll go see."

The building reminded me of something from a Steinbeck novel based in the Great Depression. Old and weatherworn, it had a wide wrap-around porch, twelve-foot-long benches on each side of the door, a hitching rail across the front of the building, and the siding had not been touched by paint in over sixty years. I opened the squeaky screen door and walked inside.

A young lady in her early twenties sat behind the counter reading a magazine. When she saw me she smiled. "Hi y'all. Can I help you?"

"Are you open?

"The season doesn't start until next week, but we're open."

"Can I get a campsite for the night?"

"Sure can!" Then she slid a registration card across the counter.

As I completed the form, she looked out the door and saw my station wagon. "Do you want a site with electricity?"

"No, all I have is a couple small tents."

"Well, you go on out there and pick yourself a campsite." She laughed and added, "They're all open."

"I'd like to buy some firewood."

She gestured towards the axe next to the door. "I don't have any to sell, but you can find some up in them woods. Just help yourself."

When I got back to my car I drove to the best campsite and set-up the tents as the kids collected firewood. Fifteen minutes later the tents were pitched, firewood collected, and supper started. While I put the finishing touches on our meal, my wife and children explored the campgrounds. They ended up at the shelter house, playing darts and shuffleboard until I called them for dinner. As the kids wolfed down their food, I noticed the distressed look on Barb's face.

"What's the matter, honey?"

"When I took the kids to the shelter house, I noticed a man looking out the window of the trailer next to the general store."

When I glanced at the green and dingy white trailer she whispered, "Don't look! He'll see you! This place gives me the creeps. Now we have a man watching us."

Using my most comforting voice I explained, "He's probably a shut-in and doesn't have anything else to do. Don't worry, it'll be okay."

As I took my first bite of food, my worried wife asked, "Do the words, 'squeal like a pig' ring a bell?"

I choked and food shot out of my mouth at the reference to a movie we had seen two nights earlier.

The kids jabbered loudly as they ate their supper but my mate and I finished our meal in silence. As soon as the dishes were done, I suggested we take a walk around the campground and see if the man was still watching.

Barb didn't like the idea, but as the children and I started walking she followed. "I'm not gonna stay here by myself!"

We made the turn toward the shelter house and my wife whispered, "He's still there."

I strained to see the man but every time I looked toward the trailer Barb would warn me not to look. A little after dark we returned to our campsite, and I built a glowing fire. We started to sing some campfire songs and everyone melted into the vacation spirit. Lost in the friendly radiance of the flames, even Barb relaxed for a while. As the kids started to settle down, I began to tell ghost stories. It seemed my audience hung on every word until a voice directly behind my wife said, "Hello folks."

We all jumped, but after the shadowy figure entered the ring of light around the fire, we realized it was the clerk from the general store.

"I'm gettin' ready to turn in. I thought I'd stop and see if y'all needed anything."

After my heart sank from my throat, I thought I'd ask the young woman about the man in the trailer. "Excuse me but my wife noticed . . . " I stopped talking as soon as

I felt an elbow dig into my ribs.

Barbara forced a smile to her face. "Uh, I noticed we might be making too much noise. We'll be a little quieter if you're going to bed."

"No, no, you folks are on vacation. You just go right ahead and enjoy yourselves."

"We're about to go to bed too," nodded Barb. "We'll see you in the morning."

No sooner than the girl melted back into the darkness, I helped our two sons into their pup tent as my wife tucked our two daughters into their sleeping bags in our tent. Before returning to the fire, I faded deep into the darkness to get a better look at the trailer window where Barb had seen the man. He was not there.

Once I noticed Barb sitting at the fire, I hurried to join her. Placing another log on the glowing embers, I whispered, "Well, nobody is watching us now."

She stared into the flames but said nothing.

"It's been a long day. We should get to bed soon. If we leave by eight in the morning, we should be in Savannah by noon," I suggested.

"Okay, but I'm going to the restroom to clean-up a

little before I turn in."

As I watched the dying coals in the fire, my wife gathered a few things from the tent and went to the showers located behind the general store. However, in a matter of moments she hurried back to my side. "I thought you said he was gone."

"I didn't see anyone."

"Well, he's still there."

I bristled, "What do you want me to do about it?" As soon as the statement escaped my lips, I realized I chose the wrong words.

"Nothing!"

How can a one-word response be so powerful? I swear I could hear the exclamation point. After a long silence I muttered, "The fire's about out. Why don't we call it a night?"

I felt the tension mount as we left the fire and slipped into our sleeping bags. Unable to doze-off, I stared at the walls of the tent as my imagination ran wild with paranoia. The eerie orange glow from the dying fire cast silhouettes of murderous backwoodsmen approaching our tent. Every sound in the night reminded me of our pending doom. Each time a twig snapped I was certain someone holding a bloody hunting knife stood just outside our tent. When an owl screeched, I knew it was someone's final blood-curdling scream. Every time fatigue forced me into a guarded slumber, I was roused by Barb's murmurs. "Did you hear that?"

During the longest night of my life, I rose to check on the boys several times. Each time I would place another log on the fire and watch it burn down to ash, laugh at my absurd behavior, get back in my sleeping bag, hear another noise, and then start the routine all over again. Finally, I heard pans clattering on our picnic table. I grabbed the flashlight and a butcher knife. This time I would protect my family from a backwoods serial killer. I stood as tall as I could in a four-foot-high tent, threw the door flap back, lunged at the murderous aggressor as I shouted, "You son-of- a . . . "

Before I attacked the Killer at Kozy Kove, I tumbled out of the tent. Falling flat on my face, I saw a pillaging squirrel disappear up a tree.

Startled out of her shallow sleep, Barb screamed, "OMG. What happened?"

"Uh, nothing. I can't sleep so I thought I'd brew a pot of coffee."

Barb joined me outside the tent as the eastern sky began to lighten, and one by one the kids woke and gathered around the morning fire. Before the sun broke above the horizon, the boys and I struck camp as my wife and daughters made a cold breakfast. We packed everything except a fresh change of clothes into the station wagon and then drove to the general store. Relieved we had made it through the night, we decided to celebrate with a hot shower before we left Kozy Kove Kampground.

Barb and our daughters headed to the women's showers and the boys and I to the men's. Still early, everyone was quiet until I broke the silence when I saw the showers. "No! No! No, not pay showers!" echoed through the hollows of central South Carolina.

Over the years, I have noticed certain eccentricities about myself. For instance, I might spend hundreds if not thousands of dollars on a vacation, but when faced with a pay shower that charges a dime for two minutes or ten minutes of hot water for a quarter, it becomes a personal challenge to spend the quarter but make sure my two sons and I all completed our showers using that one coin. Needless to say, the ten-minute shower will be used as an example of insanity for as long as my sons and I live. "Quick! Quick! Get wet! Now, you soap-up while your brother gets wet. Move over. I need to get in for a second. Quick, rinse!"

As soon as the three of us were covered in soap suds, the water shut off. "What are we gonna do?" asked my second son.

I wiped soap from my eyes and lifted my pants from the bench next to the showers. "Shoot! I'm out of change."

I offered a towel to my youngest son. "Wrap this around you and get some change from the car."

"I don't have anything on," carped the boy. "Why don't *you* get the quarter?"

I said the only thing I could think of. "Because it's your turn."

He frowned as he tried to come up with another excuse.

Not wanting to be the coin gopher, my oldest son

chimed in. "It was my turn last time."

What last time? I just made it up. I shot a fearful scowl at my youngest boy as I offered the towel a second time. "Then it's settled. It's your turn."

Without question, he wrapped the towel around his waist and retrieved a fist full of change. A couple minutes later we rinsed and dressed. The hot water continued to flow well after we returned to the station wagon. The whole absurd scene defies sanity.

The boys and I waited impatiently for another ten minutes while my wife and daughters finished their primping - they used three quarters to take their showers. *Those spendthrifts!*

Desperately wanting to put Kozy Kove Kampground in the rearview mirror, I started the car as soon as Barb slid in the front seat next to me. I stared straight ahead as I put the transmission in gear; my big brown puppy dog eyes were too embarrassed to face her. "Honey, I'm really sorry. I should have listened to you and stayed someplace else. I feel like I've ruined our vacation. Just give me a chance and I'll make sure the rest of the trip is flawless."

I pulled away from the general store and started down the lane leaving Kozy Kove Kampground before Barb responded. "I shouldn't tell you this, but when I left the showers I stopped at the window of the trailer to give that man a piece of my mind."

"Well, since we didn't get chased out of the camp by a maniac with a chainsaw, is it safe to assume he was just a disabled man stuck sitting at the window and watching anything he could see?"

Barb mumbled under her breath. "Uh, no. That wasn't it."

I looked at her face for the first time since she got in the car. It seemed she was avoiding my stare. "Well?"

"Tell him mommy," said my oldest daughter.

"Tell me what?"

"I stopped at the window, but before I could say anything I realized I had been watching a window fan."

I shouted, "A window fan?"

My wife covered her face with her hand. I couldn't tell if she was laughing or crying. "Yes, a window fan. If you look at it from this angle it looks just like a head and set of shoulders. I thought . . . "

Before she could say another word I thundered, "The fan man! Are you telling me I stayed up all night because of a window fan?"

Still covering her face, Barb's shoulders bounced as she blurted, "Yes, it was the fan man."

As we left Kozy Kove, our minds roamed free to dream about the horrific Fan Man. From that point forward, every time we took another family camping trip we always remember the fan man . . . Always watching. Always waiting.

Thom Schilling

A graduate of Hanover College, Thom worked 45 years in the transportation industry while living in 25 different places throughout North America. After retirement, he worked on developing his writing skills by completing sixteen Action/Adventure novels (The ALERT Series), and four paranormal books about a Kansas Sin Eating Farmer.

In 2022, he temporarily veered from "long" works by adding two novellas, a 22 story anthology with a mix of humor and tragedy and 35 miscellaneous short stories to his collection.

2022 - Winner of the 2022 T. A. Barron Award for Best Adult Humor Writer in his "All Smiles" Comedy Writing contest.

2023 - Thom is one of the ten finalist in the Adventure Writer Competition sponsored by the Clive Cussler Collector's Society. This year's competition received a record number of submissions from 10 different countries. The Winner of the Grand Master Award will be announced in early October 2023.

Additionally, Thom is a finalist in the "Stories Through The Ages – Baby Boomers Plus 2023" short fiction contest.

Thom and his wife have 4 children, 9 grandchildren 6 great grandchildren, and they live in Arizona.

The Way It Had to Be
By Bill Smoot

Danny was sitting on the edge of his wooden swivel chair at the newspaper office, hunched over the typewriter, using two forefingers to peck out an obituary for the day after tomorrow. It was February of 1962, the year his life would change course. He hated writing obituaries, so he did them first to get them out of the way. Marilyn had corrected the last of the galley proofs and gone home, so Danny was alone in the newsroom. The pressman and the linotype operator were busy in the back. It was nine o'clock and the press would start running at ten. The phone rang on the city editor's desk. Danny walked across the office to answer it.

"This is Jimmy Jones at the hospital. Somebody just got shot."

"Where?" Danny shouted.

"The stockyards. We just got a call for the ambulance."

Danny bolted across the office, skidded to a stop in his loafers, and then scrambled past the click-a-click of the wire machines and flung open the door to the press room. "Hold the presses," he yelled, and then he sprinted back through the office and out the front door, grabbing a notebook and his jacket.

Danny had been at the paper only six months and this was the most exciting thing that had happened. He ran eight blocks down Second Street to the stockyards, the cold night air biting his face. A patrol car had pulled onto the sidewalk, its red lights pulsing against the stock pens. Police Chief Mason was standing beside it, his hands on his hips. Another police car, its lights out, was parked in the driveway. The ambulance was just pulling up.

"Danny McDonald from the *Ledger*," he panted to Chief Mason. "What happened?"

"Hell, Danny, I know who you are. It's too late for the morning paper, isn't it?"

"No, sir," Danny answered, opening his notebook. "I stopped the presses."

"Hold your horses, Danny. This is going to take some time. We haven't even got a name yet."

Danny saw the ambulance attendant, case in hand, walking up the dirt driveway with long swift strides. Danny trotted after him. The attendant knelt over a Negro man lying on his back, held his stethoscope to the man's chest, and then lifted the eyelids and shined a tiny flashlight first into one eye and then the other. Rip Reynolds, a Marysville policeman, was standing nearby.

The attendant said to no one in particular, "I'll get a sheet. And call Dick Brooks." Brooks was the country coroner.

Danny looked at the body. On the front of the dead man's tan jacket, two large blood stains glistened in the dark. The stillness of the body was what Danny felt most, a stillness eerie and absolute. The man's legs were awkwardly bent under him, as if he had died trying to sit down. Danny felt an impulse to straighten the legs.

Danny turned to Rip Reynolds and asked if he knew who shot him.

"I did," Reynolds said. He was leaning against a holding pen, his elbow resting on the top board.

When Danny started writing in his notebook, Reynolds held up his hand. "If you want quotes, talk to the Chief."

"Why did you shoot him?" Danny asked.

"He threw a rock at me, is why. Tried to bust open my head."

The ambulance attendant returned with a sheet and covered the body. Reynolds put a cigarette in his mouth and flicked his lighter several times to get a flame. His hands shook. Danny smelled lighter fluid in the cold air. The Chief called Reynolds over to his patrol car.

There was a pay phone on the porch of the stockyard office and Danny called Kenny, the staff photographer, at home.

"Shit, Danny. Old Man Bennet will never put a photo of a dead body in the paper."

"Even if it's covered with a sheet?" Danny asked.

"Hell, no. Besides, I can't get film developed and a print made for tomorrow's paper. You're past deadline anyway, aren't you?"

"They're holding the presses. This is a big story."

"No dead bodies. Call me back if the place catches fire," Kenny laughed. "Mr. Bennet likes fire photos."

Danny phoned Mr. Bennet to report the shooting.

"I thought you might want to come in," Danny told him.

"Hells' bells, Danny. I'm in my pajamas and robe. Besides, the Chief is going to get his ducks in a row before talking to us. You can put it on page one, but put it on the bottom, two columns.

"Just two? For a killing?"

"That's what I said. You don't have enough for more than six or eight column inches. We'll do more for Thursday's paper. When we've had time to do it right."

"Can I do the Thursday story?" Danny asked.

"We'll see. Just do this one and call me back when you

have it finished. These stories have to be handled with kid gloves. I can't remember the last time a cop shot somebody."

Danny jogged back to the office and wrote the story at his typewriter. He called Mr. Bennet back and read him the story.

At approximately 9:00 Tuesday night, an unidentified Negro man was fatally shot by Marysville Patrolman Charles "Rip" Reynolds in the stock yards on Second Street. Patrolman Reynolds told the Ledger that he had spotted the man prowling in the stock yards, and when he confronted the man, the man threw a large rock at Reynolds' head. Reynolds discharged his service weapon and the man fell. He was pronounced dead at the scene by Lloyd County Coroner Dick Brooks. Further details surrounding the shooting were unknown at press time.

"That's a right good job, Danny. You got a place for it?"

"Bottom right, page one. We just have to pull a story about Khrushchev at a parade in Moscow."

"That was filler anyway."

The next morning Marilyn said to Danny, "I hear you had some excitement last night."

"I'll say. I had trouble falling asleep. I kept seeing that body on the ground."

When the pressman came in, he teased Danny about the way he had yelled "Hold the presses" the night before. That afternoon Kenny laid on Danny's desk a black and white photo of the pressman, his eyes wide with mirth, holding the press with both arms. "Hold the presses" was written at the bottom in blue grease pencil. Danny smiled in embarrassment.

A month before the shooting, Danny had seen Eddie Yates, a high school classmate, downtown wearing an army uniform. When Danny told him he worked for the *Ledger*, Eddie grinned and said, "You're a downtown man."

Danny knew what the term meant. The center of life in Marysville was downtown, and the people who worked there seemed like the glue that held things together. They were the doctors and lawyers, the nurses and secretaries, the store owners and the clerks, the pharmacist who owned the drugstore and the women who worked the lunch counter. They were as familiar to the townspeople as President Kennedy was to the nation. Eddie Yates was right: Danny was now one of them, like a single brick in a large wall. He liked the feeling, and he felt affirmed whenever he was reminded of it—as the night before when Chief Mason had said, "Hell, Danny, I know who you are." Danny had lost his father when he was in high school and his mother when he was in college. This was his chance to belong in the town as a newspaper man, not an orphan boy.

Still, a question hung over Danny, the same question that hung over every young person in Marysville: stay or go? The grandparents had been as rooted in the town as old trees. The parents grew up in the depression and survived World War II, and the secure stability of Marysville was everything they had prayed for. But Danny's generation had neither the grandparents' deep roots nor the parents' hunger for security. Danny's generation had a choice. To some the question spoke loudly; for others it remained a whisper. It was a tough question. Marysville was as comfortable as a cottage. You knew everybody. People looked out for one another. You understood how things worked. But it could be a little boring. It could feel like the people looking out for you were also peering over your shoulder. After his mother's funeral, Danny couldn't get back to college fast enough, so suffocated did he feel by people's fawning sympathy. Besides, he sensed that things were happening in the outside world, and he feared missing them. Something about President Kennedy made Danny feel challenged. When Mr. Bennet offered him the job at the *Ledger*, he accepted, unsure whether it was a victory or a surrender.

As Danny walked the two blocks to the police station, he remembered a talk he heard his last year at college. The speaker was from the NAACP and his topic was, "What Negroes want—a ten-point answer." Danny had walked in a neutral observer and walked out a sympathizer to the cause. One of the ten points was an end to police violence against Negroes. The man described incidents of unjustified killings. What if last night's shooting was just such an incident?

Chief Mason handed Danny a piece of paper. The victim was Eugene Commodore, age twenty-four, single, employed as a janitor at the cotton mill working the 10 PM to 6 AM shift.

The chief repeated the story: the man had been prowling and when confronted by Patrolman Reynolds, he threw a large rock.

"The rock missed, I guess," Danny said.

Chief Mason gave Danny a hard, slow look.

"Yes, it did," he said evenly.

"Why did he have to shoot him?" Danny asked.

Chief Mason's mouth turned down like he was chewing something bitter.

"Use your head, Danny. Was he supposed to wait until the rock knocked him unconscious so the colored man could beat his brains out?"

Danny felt his face burn.

Before returning to the newspaper office, Danny walked to the stockyard. It was sunny and cold, and the yards were deserted—stock day was Monday and today was Wednesday. Trucks entering the stockyards would drive down the dirt lane past the office and then to one of the chutes that emptied into holding pens. They might stop first at the platform scale. Eugene Commodore had been shot on that driveway, close to the office. Danny looked for the exact spot, wondering if there would be blood on the ground. A faint odor of animal manure hung in the cold air. A dog sniffed at a fence post, raised his leg, and trotted on. Danny saw no blood. Then a thought hit him. There were no rocks, large or small. How did Eugene Commodore pick up a rock if there were none around? He walked the road again, looking for rocks, and then he wandered through the rest of the stockyard. The pens were packed earth and dried manure. Tough weeds grew at the base of fence posts and around the water troughs. Danny was there an hour. If there had been a dime lying on the ground, he would have found it. There were no rocks.

He felt like a balloon was being blown up inside his chest. He wanted to run through the town shouting.

He walked rapidly back to the police station. He knocked on the milky glass door to the Chief's office. He told Chief Mason that there were no rocks in the stockyard.

Chief Mason looked Danny in the eye and said, "What's your point?"

"Well, Patrolman Reynolds' story has a hole in it, sir."

"Reynolds is a sworn officer of the law, Danny. You should be careful what you say. He thought the man threw a rock."

Danny took out his notebook and wrote down the statement. "So you're saying he *thought* the man threw a rock?

"God damn it, Danny, I'm not going to argue semantics with you. I've got work to do. Have Bennet call me if you've got any more questions."

"Is Patrolman Reynolds around?"

"He can't talk about the case, so save yourself the trouble."

By midafternoon Danny had written the story. He was writing a photo caption about the election of Rotary Club officers when Mr. Bennet, wearing his overcoat and holding his hat, dropped the story on Danny's desk. A blue-penciled X had been drawn through one paragraph:

A Ledger reporter who walked the stockyard grounds on Wednesday morning found no rocks, large or small. When asked about the apparent discrepancy between this fact and Patrolman Reynolds' account, Chief Mason referred to Patrolman Reynolds as having "thought" a rock was thrown at him. Patrolman Reynolds was not available to comment on this story.

Danny felt like that balloon inside his chest had just deflated. Mr. Bennet stood by the desk until Danny looked up.

Mr. Bennet said, "We are reporters, Danny. They are the police."

"But that paragraph—it's investigative reporting," Danny said.

"Chief Mason called me," Mr. Bennet said. "He thinks you've got a wild hair up your ass."

"Because I want to know the truth?"

"Like it or not, Danny, we're the little Marysville *Ledger*, newspaper to a town of 8,000. Especially on something like this, we have to do straight reporting. We have to be neutral."

"I don't see how it's taking sides to tell the truth," Danny said.

"Look," Mr. Bennet said, "This thing could blow up. Look at what's happening in other places. Sit-ins. Marches. The Klan. We don't want any of that here. As a paper, we can stir up trouble or we can smooth things out. For the good of the town and for the good of the paper, we need to smooth things out."

Danny left the office feeling agitated. Having to hold inside what he knew about the absence of rocks in the stockyards made him feel like he was going to explode. Maybe his decision to stay in Marysville had been a mistake.

The next morning a call came into the office that Negroes were marching on the court house. Danny stifled an impulse to let out a war whoop. He grabbed his notebook, Kenny picked up his camera, and together they ran out of the office.

When Danny and Kenny turned the corner onto Court Street, they saw a crowd of Negroes at the far end. At the sight, Danny said to Kenny, "This tickles my innards."

The Negro men wore coats and ties, spit-shined shoes, and C-crown hats. The women wore dresses of blues and purples and reds, high heeled shoes and purses to match their dresses, hats with flowers or feathers or veils. A few had brought their children, also dressed for church. There were no picket signs. They spoke in low tones and piled behind Reverend Fields into the office of Judge Slade Smith.

When the people stopped moving their feet, the room fell silent. The men removed their hats. Danny and Kenny wormed their way through the people packed into the office. Someone coughed. Judge Smith stood up behind his desk, his face flushed. Reverend Fields addressed him in a sonorous voice that everyone could hear. His tone was respectful.

"We have come here not to cause a disturbance, but to ask

for justice," he began. He had a deep, soothing voice. He emphasized that the dead man had been unarmed and had not been caught breaking and entering or committing any other crime. "It is our understanding, Your Honor, that an investigation by a grand jury is an appropriate response in a case like this, be the victim black or white."

Judge Smith cleared his throat and said that he understood their concerns and appreciated their promise not to create a disturbance. Danny took notes. Kenny stood on a window sill and Danny steadied his legs while he took photos. Judge Smith told the group that yes, the law did allow opening a grand jury investigation, but that it would take time to decide whether that was appropriate in this case.

"I'll have to cogitate on it," Judge Smith said.

Reverend Fields nodded, thanked him, and led his flock onto the sidewalk where they bowed their heads while Reverend Fields prayed for the Judge's ability to accomplish justice. Then they quietly walked back toward the colored section of town. On the sidewalks, white people stopped and stared.

As Danny started back down Court Street, Chief Mason opened the door to the police station.

"Come on in here, Danny," he said. "I've got something to show you."

Danny followed him to his office, and Chief Mason lifted a jagged chunk of concrete from his desk. "This is what the colored man threw at Reynolds."

He handed it to Danny. It was as heavy as a bowling ball.

"Where was it?" Danny asked.

"Just off the driveway in the stockyards," Chief Mason said.

"Who found it?"

Chief Mason paused. "One of our patrolmen."

"Was it Reynolds?"

Chief Mason looked Danny in the eye and said, "Yes, it was."

Danny met his gaze.

"It's a huge piece of concrete that I somehow didn't see," Danny said. "I must need glasses."

"Maybe you do," Chief Mason said, lifting his chin.

Danny set the chunk back on the chief's desk with a thud. "Wouldn't be easy to throw that. Maybe the man did shot put in high school."

Danny wrote up the story of the Negroes converging on the Court House. Mr. Bennet told him it was a good story. As if to justify the paper, Bennet added, "We're running a photo of the Negroes at the Court House. Write a caption for it."

Danny did feel pleased that he was getting to write these stories. It made him feel like a brick in the town wall. Maybe the Negroes' protest would pull the paper into the controversy.

Two days later Judge Smith announced that he was convening a grand jury. Danny felt exuberant. Town gossip was that Chief Mason was livid and had a shouting match with Judge Smith on the court house steps. Danny asked Mr. Bennet if he was surprised at Judge Smith's decision.

"At first I was surprised—real surprised—but then I thought about it. Slade Smith is nobody's fool. He gave the Negroes what they wanted, and you can bet they will vote for him in the next election, but what gets decided is up to the grand jury—and Houston Royce, the prosecutor. So whichever way it goes, no one can blame Judge Smith."

"How do you think it will go?" Danny asked.

"The grand jury won't indict him."

"Why not? That shooting was real suspicious," Danny said.

"The way grand juries work is that the prosecutor pretty much leads them. And Houston Royce won't want to prosecute this case. He'd catch hell from people, and he could never win anyway."

"Why couldn't he win?"

Bennet waved his hand. "No case. Only two people know what happened that night. One of them is dead and the and the other is a cop."

The next day Danny stopped by Houston Royce's office.

"I'm not here as a reporter," Danny said. "Just as a private citizen." He told Houston Royce about carefully searching the drive in the stockyard and finding no rocks—or a chunk of concrete. He tried to read Mr. Royce's face while he was telling his story, but he couldn't.

Houston Royce put his elbows on his desk and picked up a pencil and used it as a pointer as he talked. "This is called testimonial evidence, Danny, but it's testimony about what you did not see, not about what you did see. So it's weak. If this were to go to trial, I might need you. But for a grand jury inquiry, I most likely don't need this."

Danny frowned.

"I knew your father, Danny. He was a good man, and I can see you take after him. It shows good citizenship that you came by to tell me this."

Danny left without understanding why Royce didn't need his statement.

The city editor came down with the flu, so Danny took over the front page, everything subject to Mr. Bennet's approval. Some of the lead stories those weeks were national. John Glenn was given the largest ticker-tape parade in history. Jackie Kennedy had a thirty-minute meeting with the Pope in Rome. Wilt Chamberlain set a record by scoring 100 points in a game, but Mr. Bennet moved it to the sports page. Marysville High School won the district basketball tournament, and Mr. Bennet moved that from sports to the front page.

The next week the grand jury reached the decision not to indict. That night Danny warmed up his favorite TV dinner— ham with raisin sauce—but couldn't eat it. His stomach was clenched like a fist. What of "truth, justice, and the American way," like on *Superman*? Didn't anybody in the town care about that?

Sitting on the edge of his desk, Mr. Bennet told Danny that the mere fact of the grand jury was a victory for everyone. "Indictment or not, that means something," he said. "It means we are not Mississippi. It means the concerns of the Negroes were not ignored. Hell, Rip Reynolds was sweating it. Otherwise, he wouldn't have gone back and planted that chunk of concrete."

Danny and Mr. Bennet looked at one another, both startled.

"I guess that slipped out," Bennet said quietly.

"So you agree with me," Danny said, feeling strangely moved.

Bennet looked at the floor for a long moment. "Hell, Danny, I don't know what happened that night in the stockyards, and neither do you. If I had to bet—and this is just between you, me, and the gatepost—I'd guess that Rip Reynolds, who everybody knows is a hothead, pulled the trigger when he shouldn't have. And you were smart to raise that point about the chunk of concrete. Rip Reynolds saying he found it later was like a kid stealing a candy bar and then saying it fell into his pocket."

Danny said, "I just wish we had published that paragraph about no rocks in the stockyard. So people in town would know."

Mr. Bennet stood up and walked to the front widow. The

blinds were closed. He pulled one of the slats up and looked out. With his back to Danny he said, "I know you learned about investigative reporting in college, Danny. And you know something? You might be right. If you gave that paragraph to your journalism professor, he might give you an A. If you were a reporter at the *Courier-Journal*, it might have been printed."

Mr. Bennet let the slat drop and said, "Looks like it might snow."

He walked back to his desk and sat down.

"You're a bright boy and a good reporter, Danny. In twenty years you could be editor of this paper and then you'll have to make the kinds of decisions I do. You'll have to rein in some young reporter from going too far, like I do with you. That's just the way it is."

"I know that's the way it is," Danny said, "but is that the way it has to be?"

The next day Danny was eating lunch at the drugstore counter when he overheard the conversation of three downtown men sitting in a booth behind him. They were talking about the grand jury decision.

"What I can't figure out is what he was doing in the stockyards," one of them said. "Nothing there to steal."

"Maybe he had to take a piss," another said.

"One thing's for sure. Rip Reynolds stopped him cold."

The three men chuckled.

Danny left his sandwich half eaten and walked back to the

office. Sitting at his typewriter, he thought back over his articles on the shooting, and it struck him that he had written nothing about Eugene Commodore himself, not even about his funeral. He felt a wave of shame. He had gotten so wrapped up in fighting for the truth about the shooting that he had forgotten its victim. He had ignored Eugene Commodore.

When Danny got home that afternoon, he lay on his bed and stared at the ceiling. A strange feeling washed over him, an exhaustion of the spirit so great he wasn't sure he could get up. His six months at the paper had begun with energy for learning the job. He was excited at becoming a downtown man, a brick in the wall. His excitement intensified when he tried to become a truth warrior, wanting to use his pen like a sword for justice. But that mission had collapsed in failure, and now he felt not like a downtown man but an alien visitor who did not belong. He felt like a town changeling.

He awoke that morning with a plan, as if it had crystalized in his sleep. He drove to the Negro section of town where he spent several hours gathering information. Then he went to the office and wrote an obituary for Eugene Commodore. Eugene had graduated from the Negro high school two years before the schools integrated. He was starting forward on the basketball team. He joined the army and did a tour in Germany, attaining the rank of corporal. He lived with his mother and worked as a janitor at the cotton mill for two years. He had an older sister who was married. He planned to travel to Detroit in a few months and stay with a cousin while he looked for a factory job in the auto industry. His friends said he always had a smile for everyone. In the summer he liked to fish in the river.

When Danny finished, he rolled two pieces of paper into his typewriter with a sheet of carbon paper between them. He carefully pecked out a polished version of the obituary. He put one copy in an envelope and addressed it to Eugene's mother. He considered giving the other copy to the linotype operator on Sunday and letting Mr. Bennet read it in Monday's paper, but that was too low-down a thing to do, even for a righteous cause. After all, Mr. Bennet had given him the job and treated him well. Danny would just leave the obit on Mr. Bennet's desk to serve as his letter of resignation. The obituary would be Danny's exit ticket from Marysville.

Danny realized there was nothing noble in what he was doing. If anything, leaving town was the coward's way out. He could choose to stay and fight the long fight. But he felt in his gut that this town was no longer his town, nor this life his life. On Sunday morning, he packed his car and drove west on Highway 68.

Bill Smoot

Bill grew up in Maysville, Kentucky, a child in the fifties and an adolescent beginning to come of age in the sixties. He went off to college and grad school, committed himself to the causes of the day, and then moved to Berkeley, a distance from Maysville not measurable in miles. He has spent his working life as a teacher, and left his day job in 2018 to realize his lifelong dream of becoming a fulltime writer. Bill's first project was a series of shorts stories set in a fictionalized version of his hometown during the late fifties and early sixties. He thinks of them as love letters to the place where he grew up.

Bill has written a nonfiction book, *Conversations with Great Teachers*, and published short stories in such literary journals as *The Literary Review, Crab Creek Review, and Ninth Letter*. He does pro bono teaching at San Quentin Prison.

Grace
By Elizabeth Taylor-Mead

When she looked at the wedding photograph of her long dead grandmother, she felt she could actually touch the woman's skin. The dark serious eyes under the veil's seed pearl cap pulled Abby into the sepia image, inviting her to stroke the rounded cheek of the Byzantine icon face.

She'd looked at this picture many times before, but it still intrigued her. She couldn't fit together the serene presence of the woman in the photo with the stories her mother told her about life with this parent who died at age 35. On the eve of her own wedding, Abby pulled out the photo album, and carefully removed the large photograph from the black page. Glancing quickly first at the elegant young man also standing in the studio picture, Abby gave her grandfather, a favorite relative, a telepathic kiss hello, and then sat down as she focused more intently on his bride.

Grace Adams Macaluso was a wildcat…big boned, big hearted, a raucous laugh and a knife-thrower's daring. She loved Joe, her jazz musician husband and loved her children, which is why she had so many of them. Depression children, full of life!

Unlike most of the other women in the neighborhood, who also produced one baby after another, Grace wasn't a Catholic. She was a Lutheran, the agreed upon religion of her German mother and English father. Giselle and Fred Adams were married in Philadelphia, where Mr. Adams taught music. After losing a bitter dispute with John Philip Sousa, in which Sousa vehemently denied stealing a march Adams had written, the couple moved to one of the more respectable parts of Brooklyn, New York. For the rest of his life, and even though he prospered despite this injustice, every time Mr. Adams heard the strains of Semper Fidelis, the official song of the US Marines, he'd slam his fist on the nearest surface, shouting "Strike a policeman!" The only epithet he'd ever allow himself.

Grace was born in Brooklyn and the boisterous borough suited her personality. At 18, she dreamed of all the razzle-dazzle that might await her just over the bridge, and threw herself wholeheartedly into the Jazz Age. With her bobbed hair, rolled stockings, and flapper fashion dresses, she turned quite a few heads, gravitating to young men whose spark matched her own. On a sweltering day in July, while eating ice cream cones with her best friend Ivy, Grace saw a sign announcing that a Dixieland band would be playing that night at the band shell in Prospect Park. After drying the dinner dishes, it only took a medium sized white lie to get out of the house, and the price of the trolley fare to meet the man she would marry.

Joe emigrated from Sicily with his family, arriving at Ellis Island when he was four years old. It was probably during one of the many invasions of that Mediterranean island that some marauding Viking stayed long enough to imbue the Macalusos with pale skin, fair hair and blue eyes. Still, in 1920s New York, the immigration one-upmanship dance had well defined steps. Protestant trumped Catholic and Mr. and Mrs. Adams were unwilling to swallow another bitter pill by allowing Grace to marry beneath her. Her reputation in the family was for being headstrong, but she loved her parents and wouldn't purposely defy them on a matter as big as this unless she had no choice. After three months of secret dates with Joe however, something happened that sealed her fate.

One night, he took her to Coney Island to ride the Cyclone, and then to Nathan's for hot dogs with everything, washed down by mugs of root beer, On the way back to the station, they passed a flower stall in the late-night outdoor market. Among the more mundane blooms was a bouquet of white flowers, each scented with romance -- lilies, roses and gardenias. Grace tried to stop him, knowing that the price was probably more than he made in a week, but her desire to be loved that much got the better of her, and she sniffed the bouquet and kissed him all the way back to her house. The next day she asked him what time he got home, knowing the trolleys at that time of night ran less frequently. His answer seemed a little evasive to her, so she pressed him again. Reluctantly, he explained that it wasn't until after 2 am. While he was waiting at the stop, he counted his money to make sure he had enough. He realized that the boy he bought the flowers from had undercharged him. He worried that the kid might get fired if his night's tally came up short, so he walked all the way back to save the fare, and then had to walk miles to get home as he missed the last ride. All that day Grace thought about the kind of man who does something like that. Isn't that what it means to be a hero? How often does a hero come into an ordinary girl's life? That night it was Grace who didn't sleep, and a month after that, they ran away together.

Seven children later, Joe slept all day on Saturdays, exhausted between three-show nights as first trombone with the Piccadilly Rhythm Boys. Grace spent the day trying to keep the kids quiet and doing what she could to keep the family afloat. Jenny, the only girl and second oldest of the big brood, would be dressed up in her one organdie party dress, a ribbon with a big bow fastened to her too-straight brown hair, and lifted over the fence behind their tenement building to St. Ignatius, the church on the other side. Jenny's task was to pretend to be a guest at whatever wedding was going on that day, and being an Irish/Italian neighborhood, there was always a wedding going on.

Grace armed her with a silk drawstring bag, the one her own mother had given her as part of the trousseau she added to since Grace was a child, in anticipation of the wedding envisioned for her. The silver and white bridal purse was a family heirloom. She managed to abscond with it when she and Joe eloped. She planned to keep the purse tucked away in tissue paper, saving it for Jenny's trousseau, wishing that Jenny would eventually find a husband as loveable and worthy as Joe, but with lots of mouths to feed and hard times rolling through the city like thunder, it was all hands (and useful handbags) on deck.

Traditionally filled with money, gifts to the newly married couple, this magic bag was now used as a receptacle for Jenny to stuff as many sandwiches as she could fit into it before any of the real wedding guests got suspicious. She imagined herself as a character in her favorite radio show, *The Shadow*, now on clandestine assignment. "Who knows what evil lurks in the hearts of men... The Shadow knows." Smiling sweetly and trying to look a little helpless, Jenny made her way down the food table, quickly reaching for each platter, grabbing pepper and sausage rolls, corn beef and cabbage on rye, and meatballs on Italian bread, slipping them into the waxed paper bag lining the purse that dangled from her wrist.

Some Saturdays she would have liked to stay and dance. The music was so lively, and people were having such a good time, the brides in their princess dresses, the grooms looking like the older boys who delivered the ice or worked at the soda fountain down the block only dressed up and happier, and not just because it was their day off.

Back on their side of the fence, the twins, her brothers Ralphie and Ray, were waiting to catch her as she skillfully maneuvered the chain link without catching her crinoline.

Grace waited at home in the four-room railroad flat that sat on the second floor of the narrow brick multi-family building. She moved around the kitchen in her maternity smock, her latest bulge protruding from the gap in the Chinese kimono she wore. Sweet little Tommy, not quite a year old, gurgled and bounced on her hip as she stirred the macaroni and bean soup while singing Yes Sir, That's My Baby. The sandwiches would be dinner that night, the soup the first course for Sunday lunch.

Her husband's four sisters all lived in the same building, and whether through death or drifting abandon, each had lost her mate. Lucy, the youngest sister, had only one child, red-haired Emma, who would only leave her mother's anemic and exhausted side to gravitate to Aunt Grace's apartment where there was always singing, practical jokes, and ricocheting peals of laughter.

Mary was the eldest, a quiet, humorless and devout woman. She saw her burden of single parenthood in the same light as she understood the Fourteen Stations of the Cross. She appreciated Grace's good and generous heart, and said an extra 'Our Father' each night, hoping to offset her sister-in-law's peppering of curse words as she yelled at the kids, so that she might still get into heaven.

Katie worked as a laundress, bleaching, scrubbing and wringing the bed linens and shirts, of the neighborhood. At night, her aching feet propped up on a frayed hassock, she embroidered, taking in piecework for the local manufacturer of dainty handkerchiefs.

Jean liked gambling, smoking, and hard men. She'd

been married at least three times, but with each husband a no-good louse, she stopped counting and wore red to chase away the blues. She and Grace played pinochle in the afternoons, and they pretended that Grace would someday pay off her losses when she struck it rich. Jean made a little money on the ponies, and did bookkeeping for some guys in the city, piecing together enough income to pay her bills and buy all the kids in the building outfits for Christmas and their first holy communion.

One day, Grace was fed up, the temperature was rising, they were out of ice, the younger kids had heat rash and the older ones were fighting with each other. The new baby in her belly registered his own complaints by kicking her every time she tried to sit down. "OK, you brats, meet me up on the roof in ten minutes. I have something very important to tell you. Make sure you're there by noon, you're really not going to want to miss this." Quickly throwing together a very basic picnic lunch, she grabbed some blankets, tucked the little ones under her arms, and fanned herself with a newspaper while they assembled.

The tar roof smelled like burning tires. She used the blankets to make a shady lean-to on the side of the roof that overlooked the stores on Knickerbocker Avenue. Below her, people were heading home for lunch, but the heat meant that everyone was moving slowly. Handkerchiefs, waving like white flags of surrender, wiped away the perspiration of men in shirtsleeves and women with their blouses loosened as much as was decent. The church bell rang twelve times and looking up at her were the puzzled faces of a dozen children. "Well kids, I didn't want to mention it this morning, because there was no point scaring you so early in the day, but I've brought you all here because this is the best place to watch the world end, and that's what's going to happen in about ten minutes. That's right, I heard it on the radio, the whole thing is going to explode and we're going to have a birds-eye view! Now, who would like something to eat? Here, pass this around. Eat up as if it's your last meal, ha ha!"

The little ones took the food and began eating. The older children looked at each other and at Grace and she could tell they had lost their appetite. "But mama, what do you mean?" "How come pop isn't here?" "What will happen to us?" "How come nobody else knows about it?" Grace just munched on a celery stick and shut her eyes, shaking her head slowly. When she opened her eyes, she shushed them and made them hold hands. "It's just about time. Let's make one last wish and hold on tight. If you've been good up till now, you'll be fine. Only those naughty children who don't listen to their parents may have to stay behind. Hang on now and close your eyes. The last one into heaven is a rotten egg!" She opened one eye and saw that it was working. They were clutching each other's hands with their eyes clamped shut, worried expressions on their faces. "Count backwards, here we go. Ten, nine, eight..." She could feel the tension and when she got to one, she shouted "Boo!" and then burst out laughing. "Oh well, I guess I got the day wrong. Who wants to go swimming? Hey, why the long faces? You would think it was the end of the world, ha ha!"

As the children trudged downstairs again, pushing each other and hanging on to Grace's, arms, skirt, whatever they could grab, she noticed that Jenny was sulking, and shooting her dirty looks. "OK, girlie, spit it out. What's the matter, this heat make you lose your sense of humor?" Jenny began crying, silently at first, just her bony chest shaking, and then loud sobs broke through, melting her mother more than the heat. Grace handed the baby to Freddy, the oldest boy and gave him some change to buy the kids popsicles. She sat down on the cool stone landing and put her arms around Jenny. "That wasn't funny, mama. I was scared. You'd really miss us if we died, wouldn't you?" Grace kissed the top of Jenny's head, and kissed her twice on each cheek. "Honey, I'm sorry. Your mama's a little crazy, but hey, no one's perfect, right? Nothing bad will ever happen to you, as long as I'm on this earth. I promise. Let's sing a song together, just the two of us. Ready? Mairzey doats and dozey doats and little lambs eat ivy. A kid'll eat ivy too, wouldn't you?"

Elizabeth Taylor-Mead

Elizabeth has never lived in one home for more than 7 years. She's moved across the Atlantic four times so far and she's not taking bets on whether that's the final number. Always "the new girl", changing schools three times in the third grade, she was shy but learned to get her bearings more quickly with each move. She left her fundamentalist religious family the day after her eighteenth birthday to move to New York City and embrace a larger life. In her early 20s she co-founded a documentary film company in London and ran it for fifteen years. Film culture became her religion of choice, and after returning to the US with a husband and two small children, she stopped making films and began creating special community programming through cinema. She's been writing since she was a child, with no interest in publishing till now. She currently lives on the North Shore of Massachusetts, pursuing her entrepreneurial interests and wanderlust.

The Last Word
By Cheryl Velasquez

The joy a parent feels when the first born utters his or her first word is a source of parental pride and accomplishment. Often times there's a competition for the monosyllabic da-da or ma-ma. The child is fed a steady diet of sounds and syllables to increase his or her vocabulary and is often put on display to mimic a phrase resulting in laughter and surprise. Throughout the first few years, parental hearts swell with pride at their youngster's verbal success, even when the occasional slip of the tongue brings forth an off-colored, four-letter word. My grandmother believed children should be seen and not heard. My parents encouraged us to speak, but our words had to be polite and not interruptive.

Remember 1974? I don't. I spent most of it grounded, typically for talking back. Of all the words in my vocabulary, the two I used the most: *but dad*. My mother said good girls shouldn't be argumentative. I didn't see it her way. I viewed myself as competitive and I enjoyed the power of delivering the last word. Sadly, it took a lifetime to realize that life is not about winning the last word, it's about using the right words before it's too late.

~~~

One particular week, I was grounded due to inadequate grades. No extra activities, no weekend outings, and no homecoming dance. We're talking freshman year. Missing this event would be social suicide. I'd be an outcast for the rest of my life. So, I marched into the living room, stepped in front of the television, and exclaimed, "But, Dad. You're not fair."

Dad, engrossed in the television screen, leaned left. Arnold Palmer was about to sink a putt for the World Cup or the Masters or some nonsense program that had no meaning to me.

I crossed my arms and anchored my conviction. "You have **no right** to keep me home," I blurted, with all the confidence a chubby, 15-year-old girl could muster.

Dad's cold, steel gaze darted from the television fixing silently upon me. I stepped gingerly from his line of sight and sat on the couch. He returned focus to the
~~~

golf match in time to see the pimply little ball fall in the hole. His head bobbed in approval. He leaned back in his recliner, and smiled as if he were the one who sank the putt.

"You're grounded. End of discussion."

"But Dad…"

"Young lady, if I hear one more word on the subject, you'll be grounded for another month."

With wounded pride and the agony of defeat, I stomped out of the room screaming, "I hate you. I wish you were dead."

~~

"Cheryl, you *never* passed up a chance to argue. You look like Dad, you act like him and most of all you argue with him, regardless of whether you're right or wrong. Bull-headed Germans: that's what mom says about the two of you." My sister, Jody, handed me a tissue and I wiped away the tears that were running down my cheek after I recounted this childhood story, from more than twenty years ago.

Jody pointed out that this instance wasn't the only time in which my father and I had battled over grades, boys, and life in general.

"But dad never admits he's wrong," I said.

"And you never admit he's right. In fact, didn't dad say someday you'd come back to him and tell him he was right? I'd bet good money that you never did."

Our brother, Mike leaned against the white wall of the waiting room. "Will you two keep your voices down."

My siblings and I had been at the hospital for over six hours, passing the time the only way we knew how; recounting memories and bantering through our childhood. I looked down at my father's almost lifeless body resting on the sterile hospital bed. A bitter sorrow washed over me. My sister was correct. I never did say 'you are right', never apologized for my words, and God forbid, I never said 'I love you'.

Verbalizing love wasn't a common practice in my family. It's not that we didn't love each other, we just never expressed it. Outbursts, temper tantrums and strong opinions on the other hand were a common practice.

"You were incorrigible," Jody said, with a taunting

laughter in her voice.

"I had to fight to get anything. Being the oldest isn't easy," I volleyed.

"Quiet you two. Or else mom will start hollering. I can hear her now." Mike cupped his hands to his mouth. With a snicker, he mimicked mom. "CherylMichaelJoGus you settle down or else you'll all get a lickin'." We nodded at the familiar sound of our names pushed together as one unit.

Cheryl. Michael. Jo and Gus. Eleven months separated Mike and me. Two years separated Jody and Gus. The four of us were so close in age, mom referred to us as *stair steps*. Thirteen years later, along comes Chuck; a surprise addition to the family. I felt sorry for my youngest brother who had been sitting silently, in the corner chair. He didn't have our growing-up stories to share. The 'stair-steps' had grown up and moved away before he became interesting. But he loved listening to us. He laughed at every story as if it were his own.

"Tell the one about Tutti-Frutti," Chuck said. "I still don't understand why Jody got so mad."

"It was before the day of Baskin Robbins," Mike said.

"Mom took us to Dresden to order ice cream. Jody asked mom what flavor she wanted. Mom told Jody to order Tutti-Frutti."

Mike and I laughed at our shared memory of the ice cream lady scolding my sister for her order. *'There was no such thing.'*

Jody put her hands on her hips and protested her innocence. "It's really not that funny.

"What about the time when Mike took apart all of your bikes," Chuck said.

"It couldn't be helped," said Mike.

"You broke your bike and stole parts of ours," Jody said. "By the end of summer, we barely had one working bike among the four of us."

More laughter followed, more silence. We stood in thoughtful stillness and listened to the monitors track dad's unpredictable breaths. Each of our stories had been told countless times at every family gathering. As the years passed by, so did the embellishments, drama, and fabrications. I looked at my watch. "I hope Gus gets here soon. He left Cincinnati over four hours ago."

Chuck walked across the room and stood beside me.

"Cheryl, tell the one about carrying Gus up the hill to school on his first day of kindergarten."

"Why don't we wait until he gets here for that?" I said, and then added with a soft chuckle, "he hates that story."

The day-nurse pushed open the door and walked into the room. She removed the chart from the end of the bed, glanced at it and then walked over to the monitors connected to Dad's body. She pressed a few buttons, scribbled down a couple of notes and left without a word.

Mike picked up the chart and scanned it as if he understood the codes, nodding his head and wrinkling his eyebrows.

"What does it say?" asked Jody.

Mike shrugged his shoulders and placed the clipboard back on the hook. "Beats me. I'm not a doctor. But I bet whatever it says, it's Cheryl's fault."

We smiled at each other, our gaze slowly returning to dad. A snow-white beard replaced his clean-shaven face. The alabaster color of his skin matched his unkempt hair giving him the appearance of a man much older than sixty-two. He shouldn't be here. He should be on the golf course or at home arguing with me. He should be anywhere but here.

Four days earlier he had a sharp pain in his chest; his third heart attack and now he was in a coma, hooked to monitors we knew nothing about. Over ninety percent of his arteries were blocked. The doctors said it was only a matter of time before his heart gave out. His chest sucked in erratic breaths. The crisp white sheet rose up hard and fell back in rhythm with the oxygen filling dad's lungs. On occasion, he would wheeze, as if he were gasping for air, for life.

When Gus arrived, the five of us stood there for almost an hour and a half more. Each taking turns holding his hand. Each keeping watch so mom could get some rest. She didn't want him to be alone in case he woke up. Although unspoken, we all knew he wouldn't wake. He was going to die; yet no one wanted to face it. So, we stayed by his bed and did what we knew would make him the happiest; we shared our stories.

They say a comatose person can comprehend some of their surroundings. While none of us were really certain about that, we kept talking and sharing our stories until the high-pitched warning signal of the heart monitor cried out our worst fear—cardiac arrest. In a split-second chaos filled the tiny room. Doctors and nurses rushed in, and we were ushered out.

The next few minutes passed like hours. We stood huddled together, waiting. Wondering. Holding tight to one last hope that never arrived. Mom was the first person the nurse escorted in the room after they removed the final tube from dad's body. Then, one by one my brothers and sister and I said our final goodbye. There were no more monitors beeping or nurses buzzing around taking stats. There was no more laughter, no more stories. There was only one thing left for me to say. I leaned in to place a kiss on his cheek and whispered, "I'm sorry. You were right. I never wanted you to die."

We buried my dad the second Sunday of June— Father's Day.

After the funeral, mom and I sat at the dining room table. As tears rolled down my cheek, I shared with her my final moments following his death.

"Cheryl," she said, "Your dad never took the time to tell you how proud he was of you, but those last few days before he went into the coma, he sat right there, in that chair and talked of nothing but you kids. You were all he had in this world that he could call his own. He never said it to you, but he loved you; each and every one of you, in a very special way. I'm sure his only regret was not saying those words."

Several weeks after the funeral, my seven-year-old son flew into a rage because I wouldn't allow him to go on a camping trip with some friends. He stormed out of the room, yelling at the top of his lungs, "I hate you. I wish you were dead."

I smiled and said, "I love you, too."

Cheryl Velasquez

Cheryl says: Three people live in my head…the person I am, the person I want to be, and my mother. What do I do with all these voice? I write. Why? Because I can.

By day, she is a Director of Human Resources. In the evening and on weekends she soaks up Florida's sunshine, lives a tranquil life and creates art through watercolor and words. In 2016, she self-published a middle-grade fiction-fantasy called "What's in The Basement?" under the penname J.M. Berry. Her current work in progress is a historical fiction set in New York City, 1937. The main character is a burlesque dancer whose final act is so egregious she shuts down the industry. Cheryl has had a wonderful opportunity to live in Utah, California, and now Florida. But Ohio will always be home. She credits her mid-west values for keeping her humble and the voices in her head for fueling a creativity and passion in writing.

Living Springs Publishers

We hope you enjoyed this book. Please let us know what you think about it. You can leave a review on Goodreads, or wherever you purchased the book.

This is the seventh edition of our Baby Boomers Plus contest and book. The number of submissions to **Stories Through The Ages Baby Boomers Plus** has increased dramatically over the seven years we have held the contest. Each story is read by at least three judges. We receive stories from people just starting to write and from those who have won many awards. The competition is intense, and the judges agonize over their choice, realizing the heavy burden of being fair but decisive. There are winners and losers, that is the nature of a contest. We thank each and every author for the stories they submit and urge everyone to keep writing.

You can find information about our contests and where to buy our books at:
www.LivingSpringsPublishers.com.

Living Springs Publishers is a family owned, independent publishing company based in Centennial, Colorado. Our mission is to help authors, regardless of age or experience, share their gift of writing. Using our expertise in editing and publishing we help our clients bring their stories and manuscripts to life.

www.ingramcontent.com/pod-product-compliance
Lightning Source LLC
Chambersburg PA
CBHW071216210726
48293CB00002B/456